THE BIG SCORE

K. J. PARKER

SUBTERRANEAN PRESS 2021

First Edition

ISBN
978-1-64524-000-6

Subterranean Press
PO Box 190106
Burton, MI 48519

subterraneanpress.com

Manufactured in the United States of America

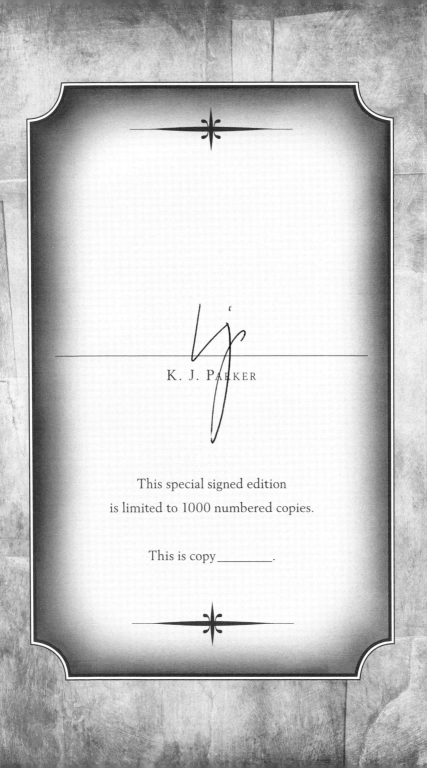

K. J. PARKER

This special signed edition
is limited to 1000 numbered copies.

This is copy _____ .

THE BIG SCORE

I didn't enjoy my funeral nearly as much as I thought I would. I'd been looking forward to it, but it turned out to be something of a disappointment.

For a start, it rained, and that always takes the edge off a good party. Maybe it was the weather; there were far fewer people there than I'd anticipated, or catered for. I'd spent a lot of money I hadn't really got on good food and fine wine (and I hardly drink at all myself, now I'm dead) and the servants ended up taking most of it home with them. The preacher's eulogy was dreadful, and most of the guests who did turn up proved to be representatives of my creditors or various law enforcement agencies. Nobody from the universities, the theatres, the Sashan embassy or the Imperial court. Instead, there was this granite-faced man with a shiny head and huge eyebrows who buttonholed me as the coffin was lowered into the hole—

"I'm his cousin," I explained. "Only living relative."

He considered me, as though I was a dangerous crack in the wall of his house. "You were close?"

I shook my head. "Hadn't seen him for years."

7

He had that expression, the one that says, you're about to lie to me. "So you've got no idea where it all is."

"The manuscripts, you mean? The research notes?"

"The money he stole."

"No idea," I lied. "Like I said, we weren't close."

"I never knew he had a cousin."

"On my mother's side," I said. "Twice removed."

ENVIRONMENT AND CIRCUMSTANCE; that's what makes you what you are, not what's inside. The shell, not the egg; the scar, not the wholesome flesh beneath. Take me, for shining example. I have, by universal consensus, the finest mind and the most beautiful soul that ever was. I've written the best plays and poems, the wisest and most perceptive philosophical tracts; I'm the greatest scientist of all time. My name—Saloninus, as though you needed to be told—will live forever. Nature (as I once put it) might stand up and say to all the world, this was a man.

Quite. And, given such rich and rare gifts, what did I do with them? To which I'm compelled to answer; apart from a few years when I lived quietly and comfortable on the proceeds of my groundbreaking formula for synthetic blue paint, nothing I care to dwell on. Lots of really bad stuff, mostly; thieving and swindling and issuing false coin (I was really good at that) with occasional lapses into the most deplorable kinds of violence. Not because I'm naturally bad and vicious—quite the opposite, since (as I convincingly proved in my *Ethical Dialogues*) beauty and virtue are essentially the same thing; therefore you can't create a substantial proportion of the beautiful things in the world, as I have, unless you're fundamentally good. No, it was always bad luck, mostly not having any money. And bad luck is just a slovenly way of saying environment and circumstances. If you end up living in Poor Town, always one jump ahead of the authorities, a certain category of things are almost inevitably going to happen to you, all of them miserable. You can call it bad luck if you like, but I'm a scientist.

So; if you take the good man out of the bad place and put him in a good place, where he's got loads of money and nobody knows who he used to be, you give him a chance to be himself; and that was precisely what I'd planned to do. Just one more little white lie, and everything would be just fine.

AT THE BANQUET I gave a little speech. We're here today, I said, to lay to rest Saloninus, the greatest and most original thinker of our time. How will future generations remember him, I wonder? As a scientist—discoverer of the circulation of the blood and the three laws of motion, the man who cured mountain fever and saved countless lives on three continents? Or as a philosopher, probably the greatest there's ever been, author of the *Analects*, the *Ideal Republic* and *Beyond Good and Evil*? As the man who invented the optical telescope, synthetic blue dye, truly functional indoor sanitation and a so far untested but entirely viable flying machine? As a playwright and composer—I give you six words that say it all. *Lycas and Thrasimene.* The Sixth Symphony. How can we truly say that Saloninus is dead when he lives on in every aspect of our daily lives? Half of the expressions we use in our everyday speech are quotations from his plays; and every time we flush a water closet or put on a blue shirt, we honour Saloninus the inventor. To say that a man like that could ever truly die is to anticipate a day when the human race itself will cease to exist—

I looked up and saw a row of blank faces. Not interested. Ah well.

For three days after the funeral, I was aware of deliberately inconspicuous men following me wherever I went. I'm used to that, of course, so I didn't go anywhere.

JUST AS WELL that I'd had the opportunities and the foresight to provide for myself during my lifetime, like a loving and dutiful father, so that my afterlife would be entirely different. Poverty, necessity and envy would no longer be the hammer and anvil between which I'd be shaped, and my basically good character wouldn't be warped and subverted into dishonesty and crime. All the sacrifices I'd made when I was alive, just so that I could have a better life after I was gone.

A few words in passing about honesty. It could be argued that the modest sum I bequeathed to myself had not been honestly come by. Fair enough. Now consider the truly inconceivable amount of wealth I've generated in my lifetime, none of which ever came my way. The best-selling book of all time, the *Analects*; I got sixty stuivers for it from a bookseller in Calyx, just enough to pay my arrears of rent on a damp rabbit-hutch up sixteen flights of stairs. For the plays I got an average of eighty stuivers each; less for the symphonies, and I never actually got the money for the Ninth, because the promoter went bust just before the premiere. True, I did actually get paid for inventing blue paint, but everything else—either someone else got the rights for a pittance, or I had to leave the jurisdiction in a hurry, and so couldn't hang around to argue my case in the civil courts. Now I ask you, is that fair? Is that honest?

Mine is a multifaceted character and I can't credibly deny that a lot of those facets are less than admirable. I became a crook when I was young, impressionable and broke, was forced to carry on being crooked by circumstances beyond my control, and sort of stuck like it thereafter. Another thing I'm forced to admit is that the intelligence, creativity, let's use the word, genius I exhibit in other areas of endeavour hasn't really manifested itself to any marked extent in my criminal activities. The most I can say is, I've made a lot of money and I've never done time. But I've jumped out of a lot of windows and left a lot of towns and cities in a hurry, mostly leaving my ill-gotten gains behind. My biographer says that ninety-six per cent of the money that passed through my hands in my lifetime was dishonestly obtained. Don't know where he came by that figure, but it sounds about right. So; big deal. I am (to quote me; *King Minax*, act three, scene one) a man more sinned against than sinning, and surely that counts for something.

Or does it? I could argue it conclusively either way, if you paid me for my time. In the absence of financial incentives, I'd say I don't know and I don't really care. All I know for sure is that from time to time I've found myself in dire straits, penniless and on the run, always because of something I did in the last country, or the one before that, and under those oppressive circumstances I've been forced to do things—steal things—that a flawlessly honest man would've left alone. It didn't help that I'm so smart, and honest people are, in comparison, so very stupid.

ONE OF THE problems with being dishonest is that you're forced to spend much of your life in the company of very bad people. This isn't as negative as it sounds until you reach the point when you have no choice but to trust them. And then, surprise surprise, they let you down.

"What do you mean," I said, "he's not here?"

She looked at me. She'd been beautiful once, but twenty years of being married to him had scoured her down to bare rock. "He's not here," she said.

"Then where is he?"

"Don't know."

"When will he be back?"

"Don't know."

She was lying, naturally. I could tell, because I saw her brace herself for the slap across the face, the fingers round the neck; I'd rough her up a little and then she'd tell me the second lie, which would send me racing off somewhere while she and he quietly packed up and left town, with all my money. My inheritance, from myself.

"Don't give me that," I pleaded. "Listen, here's the deal. We'll split it, fifty-fifty. That way, you and he will have enough to live on for the rest of your lives, and you won't have to spend every second of every day looking over your shoulder. It's got to be worth it to you. You can't put a price on peace of mind."

Not a flicker. "I'll tell him," she said. "When I see him."

"When might that be?"

"Don't know."

"Fine," I said. "I trusted him. We've been through hell together. I saved him from the gallows, did he ever tell you that?"

"Yes."

"The hell with it," I said, "it's only money. Enjoy it while you can. He'll have gambled it all away in five years."

"Less than that, probably."

I winced. I'd worked hard for that money. Some of it—about 0.01%—was every penny I ever earned from writing *The Consolation of Philosophy*, *Philemon and Arcite* and *The Principles of Mathematics*. The rest was the haul from the United Sword Blade Bank, where we got in through the roof using a practical application of my discovery of the square on the hypotenuse. Still, it's only money—'twas mine (quoting me again), 'tis his, and shall be slave to thousands. Besides, there was always the other stash.

To reach it meant nine days walk up the Great East Road, in dead men's shoes; scratch that, worse than dead men's shoes because I'd been buried in my only decent pair, assuming I'd only have a short stroll across the city before inheriting a small fortune. After two days on the road, with nothing to eat except nettles and nothing to drink but rainwater from ditches, I was starting to think mournful thoughts about the two gold angels I'd caused to be laid on my eyes to pay the ferryman, a superstition I've never ever believed in, but you feel the need to do these things properly, don't you, especially when it's for yourself. Two gold angels currently lying in a hole in the ground, when they could be paying my fare to Erech, first class, wine with my dinner. Only a halfwit puts respect for the dead above the needs of the living, particularly when they're both him.

Erech is a miserable place, too hot in summer, freezing cold in winter, and the rest of the year it rains. They make a ridiculous amount of money there growing flax, and a substantial part of the flax-grower's craft consists of leaving the loathsome stuff lying around in heaps until it starts to rot. The resulting perfume hits you just before you get to the *Angel of Resilience* (assuming you're coming in on the Military Road, from the west) and you don't really get used to it for another seven miles, by which point you're in the outer suburbs. Of course, long-term residents just look at you blankly and say, what smell?

I'd have stopped off at the *Angel* to rest up and cut the dust if I'd had any money and if I hadn't been barred for life for lewd behaviour (only I was dead now, so presumably that no longer applied); instead I pressed on, hoping to get to the Silver Rose monastery before they locked the gates for the night. But I cleverly put my foot in a rabbit-hole and sprained my ankle, which meant another night out in God's clean fresh air, leading to pneumonia. I ended up in the Silver Rose after all; I woke up in the infirmary, looking into the pale blue eyes of a tiny, impossibly ancient monk, who told me I nearly died three times, but he'd prayed for me and now I'd be fine. To which I think I muttered something like, I can't die, I'm dead already, which the monk quite reasonably attributed to me being off my head with fever. Later that day he came back and told me that he'd gone to all that trouble because every human life is precious, even one as pointless and inconsequential as mine. I thanked him and asked him when I could leave. Soon as you like, he told me; I'd served my purpose, enabling him to achieve divine merit by saving my life through prayer, and now I was no further use to him and taking up valuable space.

"Thank you, Father," I said. "If ever I'm rich, I won't forget what you've done."

"Bless you, my son," he said. "But I'm not holding my breath."

In the grounds of the Silver Rose there's a ruined chapel. It's about a thousand years old; the shattered arches are clearly late Mannerist, and when I first went there you could still pick out faint traces of what must have been unbearably lovely frescoes in the Rose Curtain style, though the sheep have rubbed them all away now. The chapel was built to house the tomb of Cassius Cascianus, the second-greatest (guess who's the greatest) alchemist of all time. I'd chosen the tomb to hide my reserve stash in partly as a gesture of respect to my brother scientist, partly because I know for a fact that nobody ever goes there, because they think Cassius sold his soul to the devil—which I know for a fact isn't true, for what it's worth. They're getting Cassius mixed up with another great alchemist, who did just that. One of my more interesting adventures. Tell you about it some time.

I was almost right. Very, very few people ever went there. Quite probably just me and one other, and him only once, with a sledgehammer and a crowbar. He'd made a real mess, whoever he was; he'd cracked the lid, which I'd been at great pains to lift and slide away, and bashed a hole in the side, which meant the rain had got in and reduced the mortal remains of the Father of Science into stinking grey porridge. Desecrating a tomb, for crying out loud. Some people have no respect.

THEY DO SAY you can't take it with you.

Still, I have to admit, it was one of those low spots, when you can't seem to see your way forward. I guess I allowed anger to cloud my judgement, which is never a good thing. The thought that some thief, some criminal, had coolly helped himself to what I'd spent the best years of my life accumulating, bit by painful bit—graverobbing, I ask you, stealing from a dead man, how low can you get? I never did anything like that. If only he'd left some clue, I'd have been after him like a shot. But he'd been careful, left no sign or trace. I remember sitting there in the brick-dust, with the sludgy residues of Cassius Cascianus smeared up my arms to the elbows, thinking; all for nothing, all that work, all that pain. An entire life, rich in adventure, achievement and acclaim, and absolutely nothing to show for it.

Also the distressing knowledge that I'd burnt my bridges. True, being me had grown increasingly uncomfortable over the years—it's a big world, but not nearly as big as they'd have you believe, and ever since I published *The Pathology of War* fifteen years ago, there's ever so much more peace and friendly co-operation between nations, which means among other things quicker and easier extradition, so nowhere's really safe any more and it's all my own stupid fault. Even so; when I was alive, there was always some far-flung godforsaken place I could go, hole up in a garret somewhere, write a book or a play, earn a little bit of money, though never enough; always some rustic grand duke willing to keep me in bread and cheese in return for linking his name with the greatest genius who ever lived. Now that I was dead, however—

The Silver Rose gets its name from the spectacular altar piece donated to the monks by Amalrich III (praised by many as the ultimate triumph of Formalist art, though I always reckoned it was gaudy and just a trifle vulgar) which used to adorn the Inner Triclinium before somebody stole it and broke it up for scrap. Not something I'm proud of, but if they couldn't be bothered to keep it secure, they didn't deserve to have it; their pathetic approach to security had cost me everything I had in the world, so I reckon they owed me. It took me nearly a whole night to saw the bloody thing up into sections small enough to carry, and I only got a fraction of its bullion value from a thoroughly dishonest silversmith in Old Town who tried to make me believe it was only sixty-seven parts fine.

It was a good reason for leaving Erech, at any rate, and at least I could afford a ride on the stage as far as Numa, where I forged an Imperial travel warrant that got me a berth on a cotton freighter as far as Beloisa. Cotton ships don't move very fast—they don't have to—so I had a bit of time to think.

What I should have been thinking about was what I was going to do next. Instead, I allowed myself to be distracted into contemplation of the question of evil, a topic which I keep coming back to, even though I thought I'd settled it once and for all in Act 2 of *Carausio* and *Reflections On The Abyss*. Apparently not. So I thought about it some more, in the light of my recent experiences, and realised that I was gradually drifting towards a whole new set of conclusions. I remember sitting on deck with my back to the mast and my feet up on a coil of rope, struggling with the realisation that the resolution I thought I'd found ten years earlier, in the magnificently argued third section of *Human, All Too Human*, was actually just plain wrong. I'd contrived to talk myself into believing it, but once you set aside the eloquence and the passion and the sheer poetry of the argument, there was a gaping hole in the hypothesis, bigger than the hole in Cassius' tomb, and look what happened to him.

Nuts, I thought; one of the finest achievements of the human intellect, reduced to grey mush by a little clear thinking. Pity, really; and if word of it ever got out, a lot of people were going to be very disappointed. I got sixteen honorary doctorates from universities right across the world for *Human* (I was stripped of all of them, of course, for being a bad boy, but it's the thought that counts) and nobody would dare to try and pass himself off as educated or enlightened unless he's read it, and at least half a dozen of the associated commentaries; they spend a whole year on it at the Studium, and it's the only foreign language text in the syllabus of the Echmen imperial academy. And one of these days, some bright spark will come along, notice what I'd just noticed, and get rich and famous overnight reducing my glorious edifice to rubble. One more nail in my coffin; just what I needed, right then.

It could have been worse. I remember doing more or less the same thing to the celebrated mathematician Proedrus; I disproved the theorem on which his entire reputation was based. Took me about ten minutes, when I should have been working on something else, and because I was young and stupid and not inclined to consider the effects of my actions, I shared my results with the senior tutor, who arranged for them to be published. It destroyed poor Proedrus, a gentle, kind-hearted man who'd spent thirty years working on it. He resigned his lectureship, gave all his money to the university trustees and died two years later of malnutrition and despair. At least that wasn't going to happen to me. I was dead already.

Still; if it wasn't murder, it was manslaughter by reason of criminal recklessness, and trying to blame it all on the truth really doesn't cut it. The truth is a piss-poor excuse for ruining someone's life, your own or somebody else's. What is a truth, a fact, but a hypothesis that hasn't been disproved yet? Until I stuck in my oar, Proedrus' theorem was a fact, true, the truth; likewise the detailed account of the wanderings of the Chosen People in the first five books of Holy Scripture, until some clown (go on, guess) happened to point out on purely philological grounds that they must've been written at least five hundred years later than they claimed to be, and some halfwit (you're way ahead of me) translated the three-thousand-year-old inscriptions on the ruins of Louada which proved that the Children of the Sun never were slaves in Blemmya and far from conquering the Promised Land, they'd been living there all along. That particular snippet of truth started two major wars and deprived countless thousands of people of a faith which was the only thing that made sense of their unbearably miserable lives. Show me a lie that ever did that much damage.

So; I had no duty to the truth; screw it. On the other hand—

"LET'S GET THIS straight," he said. "You claim you've written a book that *disproves* Saloninus' theory of the origins of evil?"

"Yes," I said. "And it's yours for one thousand angels. Cash," I added quickly.

He nodded. "And who are you, precisely?"

"Me? Oh, I'm just a wandering scholar. Just so happens I've devoted my life to the study of this particular area of ethical theory, and—"

"You're a professor? Which university?"

"No, I just said. I'm a wanderer. I move from city to city, consulting all the great libraries."

"How many books have you published?"

"None. None yet. Of course, this book will be—"

He was looking at me. "Just to recap," he said. "You're not a professor, and you haven't published any books. Nobody's ever heard of you. I certainly haven't, and I'm pretty well informed, I have to be, it's my job. That's what you're telling me, isn't it?"

"More or less."

"I thought so. What in God's name makes you think anybody will be interested in anything you have to say?"

I opened my satchel and pulled out the manuscript. "Read it," I said. "It's all in there. Once you've read it—"

He shook his head. "You're nobody anyone's ever heard of and you're asking people to believe you know better than *Saloninus?* Oh, please."

"I knew him," I said.

"Saloninus?"

I nodded. "We were really close."

"Somehow I doubt that."

"I was with him at the end. I paid for his funeral."

He sighed. "It may interest you to know that Saloninus has been dead for seventy years. That's a *fact*. Look it up."

No point arguing, so I left. Nor did I argue with any of the twelve other booksellers I tried to interest in my manuscript, all of whom said the same thing. In the end, I sold the bloody thing to a student I met in a bar; he was out getting drunk, he told me, because he couldn't face the thought of his tutorial with Professor Venhart in two days time, when he'd be forced to admit that he'd been unable to make head nor tail of *Human All Too* bloody *Human* and therefore was in no position to render a reasoned critique. Funny you should say that, I told him, and shortly afterwards a gold angel changed hands. One angel.

("It's sodding long," the student said.

"Value for money."

"I can't copy out all that, I'll sprain my wrist. Can't you sort of cut it down a bit?"

"Every single word in that has been chosen with the utmost care and precision. Take out anything and you'll ruin the structured procession of the argument."

"Oh balls.")

You CAN EXIST for quite some time on one angel, if you don't mind oatmeal porridge. And the porridge life has this to recommend it. You get plenty of time to think.

So I did that; and a fat lot of good it did me. Properly speaking, now that I'd demolished the basic foundations of the modern consensus on the origins and nature of evil,

I should've applied my mind to figuring out something to replace it, but I thought, can I be bothered? Answer; no. Instead, I went a certain way towards a scheme for defrauding the Consolidated Goldsmiths' Bank by means of leveraged derivatives based on ultimately worthless mortgages on derelict and abandoned properties. It would probably have worked, at least long enough for me to scoop up the money and run—which was why I didn't bother with it. The thought of the running part of it made me feel tired. The whole point of my death and resurrection was that I wouldn't have to run any more. And since my death, apart from the little matter of the Silver Rose, I'd been as guiltless as a novice in a convent. Did I want to jeopardise all that simply because I was starving and sleeping in doorways?

One such doorway led to the auction rooms in Blind Eye Yard, and I was woken up there very early one morning by a irritable porter who wanted me to move before the bidders started arriving. Turned out that today was a big day for the auctioneers. There was only one lot; the original manuscript of *Philemon and Baucis*—

"By Saloninus."

The porter looked at me. "Fancy you knowing that."

"Everybody knows *Philemon and Baucis*."

He nodded. "Even the likes of you," he said. "Anyway, they've got hold of it and they're selling it today. Going to be the biggest sale we ever did," he went on. "They're expecting buyers from all over the world, Scheria and Echmen and God only knows where. We had to lay on extra chairs."

"So it's valuable?"

He looked at me as if I was simple. "Half a million angels," he said. "That's the *reserve*."

I walked away feeling like I'd been run over by a dray. I can clearly remember writing *Philemon and Baucis*—which is, if you ask me, a trivial piece of fluff which flirts with a few interesting issues of identity and integrity but never really addresses them. I dashed it off in a tearing hurry after three months agonising over a much better play which I just couldn't get into (a year later it became *Vetranio*, so I was quite right not to screw it up by writing it when I wasn't ready) and I think the only time I actually read it was when I made the fair copy, which I wrote out on the backs of ninety copies of a proclamation about public sanitation, which some fool carelessly left scattered about the city, nailed to temple doors.

Half a million angels. Five hundred thousand times more valuable than my refutation of Saloninus' doctrine of evil.

(Talking of which, I happened to run into that student again when I was begging on the Priory steps. I want my money back, he said. Really? Yes, he said. That bloody essay you sold me. I got a C. That's impossible. No it bloody isn't, he yelled in my face, and I came this close to getting slung out of the university for presuming to cast doubt on fundamental doctrine. You might have warned me, he said. If I get sent down, my dad'll kill me.)

FIVE HUNDRED THOUSAND angels. And not for the play, just for *one copy* of it.

I tried to remember what had happened to it, after it was grabbed out of my hand by an angry manager, who told me it had better be good since I'd left it so late he hadn't got time to read it. Presumably it ended up on a shelf or in a trunk. Then somebody found it, realised it might be worth money, sold it to someone who sold it to somebody else who sold it to somebody else. Now, with Saloninus dead, the supply cut off for ever and ever, the time had come to realise an exceptionally valuable asset, before the world had had time to consider Saloninus carefully and dispassionately and make up its mind whether he really was such hot stuff after all.

That word valuable. A thing having value. Define value. Value is what, all things being equal, somebody is prepared to pay. And thereby hang all the law and the prophets.

I borrowed some clean clothes from someone's negligently guarded washing line and went to the auction. I sat on my hands in case anyone misconstrued an unguarded flinch as a bid. The room went really quiet when the bidding approached one million, and when the hammer finally fell everyone started to cheer, as though something worthwhile and noble—something valuable—had just been achieved, whereas all that had happened was that a proxy for a very wealthy aristocrat from Choris Seautou had paid a silly price for ninety sheets of stolen Government paper. I felt like I'd been robbed.

To MARK THE glorious victory of the Choris nobleman, and because the heightened public interest was terrific for business, the Admiral's Men put on a brand new production of *Philemon and Baucis* at the Cockpit, which I duly attended. I'd never actually watched the play before, and my view was a bit circumscribed (I had to prise up a flagstone round the back of Haymarket and crawl through a disused sewer; otherwise they wanted me to pay them three stuivers, just to see my own play) but my original low opinion of the work remained broadly unchanged. I could write something like that standing on my head, I thought—confidently, since I already had.

It had been a while since I'd written a play. Some nations have a rich and vibrant theatrical tradition, others prefer to watch chariot races and bullfights, and in recent years circumstances had landed me in sporting rather than literary jurisdictions—no bad thing; you can wager on fights and races, but nobody's going to bet you money on the outcome of a play. Still, I thought; if I can do it, it can't be that hard. I raised a month's porridge money by selling the clothes I'd borrowed to go to the auction, and fortuitously the city authorities had just issued a new proclamation about grain prices or something such; ink you make from soot, and a pen is just a matter of sneaking up on the nearest goose. I found a shady place under the aqueduct arches where nobody goes because of the smell, and tried to think of something to write about. No dice.

THE PRIORY STEPS is probably the best begging pitch in this man's town. You get people with money and consciences—cause and effect, presumably—delighted to buy a little peace of mind for less than the cost of a cinnamon biscuit. Goes without saying, I had no right to be there. You have to pay the Guild a small fortune for a square yard of the steps, and if I had that kind of money I wouldn't need to beg. But it so happened that the rightful occupant of the fifth step down on the left was indisposed after eating something that disagreed with him (don't look at me, I was the other side of town when he actually ate it) and wasn't able to attend to business for a week, during which time I claimed squatter's rights, so to speak. I got a lot of filthy looks from the other pitch-holders, but since I was being blind from birth for professional reasons, I could quite justifiably pretend not to notice.

To be blind from birth on the Priory steps, you wear a strip of dirty bandage over your eyes; even so, I really should have seen her coming a mile off.

"Hello," she said, about two feet over my head. Actually, it was hello followed by a name I hadn't heard in a long time, which happens to have belonged to me once. I winced.

"Go away."

I heard a coin clink in my hat. "I've been looking for you. You're hard to find."

"Not hard enough, evidently."

I felt a slight pressure against my shoulder as she sat down next to me. Made my skin crawl. "Everyone thinks you're dead."

I sighed. Prophets and holy men get rich and famous for acts of resurrection, but it's not always a helpful thing to do. "They're right," I said.

"Of course they are." She paused. "Little job I want you to do for me."

THE LAST TIME I saw her, I had this ghastly ringing in my ears, mainly because I'd just combined *sal tonans, aqua regia* and *aqua fortis* in a small glass bottle and dropped it off the roof of the sixth precinct Watch house in Beal Defoir—an injudicious thing to do, as you'll know if you've studied alchemy, unless you actually want to blow a hole in a wall big enough to drive a wagon through.

I didn't want to blow holes in the Watch house, not one bit. It's illegal, and it meant I had to leave town in a hurry. She made me do it. She's made me do a lot of things, over the years.

If I hadn't done it, she wouldn't have escaped from her cell, and they'd have taken her out into Cartgate and strung her up; and the world would have been a better place, if a bit less lively. But she'd looked at me with those endless grey eyes and reminded me of various things we'd done together, which (up to then) she'd never told anyone about; in consequence of which, I spent a truly horrible night distilling seven grains of *sal tonans* on makeshift equipment over a charcoal stove; one careless move and they'd have had to redraw all the City maps. It was people like her I'd died to get away from, but apparently, what we had together endured beyond the grave, just like true love is supposed to do.

"Well?" I said.

"Nice to see you too." She scowled at me. "You bastard. I was *heartbroken.*"

The thing is, sometimes she tells the truth, and sometimes you believe her. "Not for long."

She shook her head. "I had you dug up."

I opened my mouth but nothing came out.

"Well," she said, "I had to know for sure. Who was he, by the way?"

"No idea. Just someone I found in the river."

"I didn't tell anyone," she said. "Yes, that's him, I told them. He didn't look a bit like you."

"Cremation next time," I said.

"How could you? I cried buckets."

I looked at her. "What exactly do you want?"

"Nothing much. I don't know how I managed to keep going, thinking you'd died. It was like the world had suddenly ended."

"Nothing much?"

"I need you to kill the Lurian ambassador."

SHE'S NOT BEAUTIFUL by any definition, but she's one of those people you can't help looking at when she walks into a room. It's like all the strings were loose until she came along, and just by being there she tightens and tunes them. Please note that I haven't specified the kind of string.

She told me once she comes from Luria, but I don't think it's that simple, because nothing about her ever is. Don't ask me how old she is; I've known her for twenty years, but she hasn't changed a bit. She can't sew a straight line or boil an egg, but she does the very best fake cursive minuscule money can buy, good enough to fool all the scholars in the Studium, as she's proved over and over again. She told me once, a forgery's got to be better than the real thing if you want to fool anyone—painting, coinage, sculpture, manuscript, whatever. I guess that makes her the best creative artist who ever lived, because she's faked them all in her time.

"You must be getting me muddled up with someone else," I said. "I don't kill people."

She smiled.

"Except in the last extremity, in self defence," I said. "And that was years ago."

That got me her cool look. "Your wife," she said.

"I'd forgotten about her. But that was an accident. Really an accident."

"And then you killed twenty-seven people in an explosion, including the Grand Duke."

"Self defence."

She didn't actually smile, but her lips warped a little bit. "Well, this'll be self defence too. Because if you don't do it, I'll turn you in and they'll hang you. Self defence once removed."

When I first knew her, she made me do dangerous, immoral, illegal things just by being beautiful at me. We'd come a long way since then.

WE WENT TO the *Sun in Splendour*, where they really aren't fussy, and I bought Vesani retsina for her and a small peach tea for myself. There's a sort of balcony on the third floor. You get a breathtaking view out over the Bay, and the only possible eavesdroppers are spiders.

"Why do you want me to kill the Lurian ambassador?"

She smiled at me. "It was a long time ago," she said. "I was fifteen, he was seventeen, we were very much in love. We sat on the beach at twilight. He swore he'd never forget me, as long as he lived."

Starting to make sense. She hasn't changed a bit in all the years I've known her, that's for sure. Good chance, therefore, that her girlhood sweetheart would recognise her if he saw her again; and when I was still alive there were more outstanding warrants against me than her, but not that many. "Why not simply leave town?" I asked her.

She shook her head. "It's the big score," she said, and even though I knew her so well, the low hiss in her voice thrilled me. "Really, it is. The one and only. If it goes through, we'll never have to work again."

OH, THAT.

The big score. The ultimate caper. The very last and the very best. If it actually comes off, all your troubles will be over, money will flow like rivers when the snow melts, the rest of your life will be a symphony of sweetness and joy and you'll have proved beyond a shadow of a doubt that it *was* all worthwhile, that you were right to spend your life and your talents on this side of the fence, that it wasn't all a horrible mistake and a tragic betrayal of everything you might otherwise have been. And it comes only once in a lifetime, until you screw it up and barely escape by the skin on the backs of your heels, and the week after next you start off all over again with another big score or ultimate caper.

But the trouble is, you *have faith*. It's like falling in love. You know full well, when the first poison tendrils hit you and start winding themselves through your heart-strings, that it's all a mistake and it can only end in tears, but what the hell, you can't help it. It's not a rational, informed choice. You see, and you *believe*.

Blessed are those who have seen and yet have not believed; but the blessed in this context are few and far between. Personally, I think the idea of the big score calls out to the inspired part in us, the part wherein dwell all those wonderful wasted gifts and talents we live by perverting and abusing; every master needs a master-piece. You can spend thirty years painting a hundred and twenty portraits of noblemen's prize racehorses, or you can be Prosper of Schanz and use up the same length of time creating just one colossal bronze horse. The race-horses will pay better, in the long run, but the bronze horse will be a keystone of men's souls until the sun goes cold. Also, with the big score, you get all the money at once, which means you can stash it somewhere safe, turn into a dragon and sprawl all over it till you rot.

"TELL ME ABOUT it," I said.

She shook her head, which made the ends of her hair swing like bells. "I know you, remember?"

She thought that if I knew what the game was, I'd dart in ahead of her, do the scam myself and cut her out. The thought never crossed my mind, though it may have hung in the air overhead like the sun.

"Fine. You need the ambassador out of the way so he won't recognise you. Does he actually have to be dead?"

"I ask you to do one simple little thing for me, and all I get is attitude."

"Killing people makes things complicated," I said. "More difficult, not less. If an ambassador suddenly drops dead, people ask questions. The whole point, I'd have thought, is to avoid curiosity."

"Not if he dies in his sleep of a heart attack."

Diamonds are proverbially a girl's best friend, but she was also on excellent terms with foxgloves. As well as being an outstanding artist, she has a thorough grasp of practical alchemy, an encyclopedic knowledge of the herbiary and a rock steady hand. A girl who's never happier than when she's among the flowers.

"All right," I said. "Why me? I don't know the man. I don't mix in those circles. You obviously do, or you wouldn't be scared stiff of bumping into him. You do it."

"I might get caught."

I breathed in deep, then out again slow. "It works both ways, you know. I could tell on you."

She beamed at me. "You'd never do a thing like that."

"Don't be so sure. When they're pulling out my teeth with blacksmith's tongs and asking me who put me up to it, I could say all sorts of things."

"Tell them the Blemmyans paid you to do it. They'd love that."

"You tell them."

"No thanks. Why keep a dog and bark yourself?"

"I don't know the man," I repeated.

"I'll get you an introduction."

"Why me?"

She gave me a smile like a sunrise. "Because this job's really difficult and suicidally dangerous and you're the smartest and most resourceful man who ever lived, of course."

"Ah."

IF YOU WANT to learn a profession, I heartily recommend being on the run from the authorities. You're holed up somewhere, in a derelict barn or an abandoned warehouse, and all you have with you by way of entertainment, spiritual guidance and self-improvement is one book.

In my case, *Principia Medica*, by Aimeric de Poulignac. I stole a luxury edition of it many years ago from the treasury of the Golden Wing monastery at Scell, along with a sackful of other trifles. During the course of the proceedings, I got in the way of a crossbow bolt loosed off by a careless watchman. I managed to get as far as the harbour, where I had a fishing-boat tied up ready and waiting to take me to Steepholm, a small uninhabited island about three miles off the coast, where there's a ruined priory, an ideal place to stash my modest haul while I made enquiries among wealthy art-lovers. I got to Steepholm, and crawled on my hands and knees to the ruins, and after that things are a bit vague. I remember waking up in a shirt brown and sodden with blood to find eight inches of oak dowel sticking out of me, and not feeling myself.

I hadn't set out to steal the book; it was dark in the treasury and I scooped things up at random and shoved them in the sack, until the barking of unpleasant-sounding dogs made me think it was probably time to go. It was only when I opened the sack, hoping to find something I could use to mop up the blood, that I saw the gold lettering on the gold-and-jewel-encrusted spine. What a pity, I'd been thinking, that there isn't a doctor around, he might possibly have saved my life—and then, lying half-covered by the burlap, not a doctor but the thing that makes doctors; the standard work, the set text, everything you need to know about repairing the human body between two vulgarly ornate covers. It was as though I'd been starving and crying out for bread, and stumbled on a two hundredweight sack of flour.

Poulignac wrote in Old High Scherian and the book has no index, but eventually I found the bit about extracting arrows and more or less figured it out; Old High Scherian isn't that different from Melgoil, and if you can understand Pausanee, you can sort of burst your way through Melgoil, like a pig in an outhouse. In retrospect

I realise that I guessed some of the words wrong. I was fine with the introduction (I clearly recall the statement, "arrows inflict wounds with a fatality greater than that of other weapons, particularly when surgical assistance cannot be obtained") but after that it got a bit technical, and I had to keep flicking back to the anatomy section, with my finger between the pages to keep the place. Still, Poulignac saw me through, more or less. He warned me that muscle contraction can be strong enough to bend the point of the arrow, so press down a tad before pulling up—sure enough, he was right; the horrible thing had missed the bone, thank God, but the tip was bent up into a hook, which would've ripped me open if I hadn't disentangled it first. Fortunately I trusted him when he told me to enlarge the wound channel slightly to aid extraction. I really didn't want to, because it meant pushing the pin of a big gold brooch I found in the sack all the way down the wound until I felt the end of the arrowhead, and prising the hole open to make that extra bit of room, but I did it anyway and thereby saved myself from the horrors of pulling out the shaft and leaving the head still in there. All in all, the whole business went surprisingly smoothly, and the worst thing that happened was blood getting all over the exquisitely illuminated pages of the book, thereby significantly reducing its value to collectors.

After that, fever set in, as Dr Aimeric had warned me it would, and after that I was as weak as a kitten for a long time, with nothing to do but lie very still and catch up on my reading. By the time I left the island, I reckon I knew as much about the science of medicine as most of the people who earn their living from it, and very useful that knowledge has been to me over the years. It was only later, during a period of enforced isolation in a condemned foundry in Mesembrocea, that I realised that Poulignac had been wrong about quite a few things, which led me to research this and that, which resulted in my own *Praecepta Medica*, which they tell me has pushed Poulignac out at most of the leading schools, and for which, incidentally, I never got a bent trachy in royalties.

Long story short; I make a pretty convincing doctor when the need arises, so when we were trying to figure out how to worm me into the palace so I could murder the Lurian ambassador, I suggested she introduced me as the learned Dr So-and-so, professor of medicine at the Echmen Imperial University.

Echmen doctors are the best in the world, and I decided I was one of them. I happen to like the Echmen—pity I can never go back there, really—and their language is actually quite simple when you get into it. She kindly offered to act as my translator—she does actually speak Echmen, believe it or not, one of about twenty people in the West who can; but we had reason to believe that one of the remaining eighteen might be hanging around the Court at that time, so we decided to play it safe. As a doctor, of course, I could poison who the hell I liked, and nobody would be ill-bred enough to comment.

I'd been professor So-and-so before, so I knew him quite well. I think he actually exists somewhere, hence my reticence with his real name, though if he's still alive he'd be an old man now. The version of him I created was court physician for a while to the Count of Auvade—during which time I took the opportunity to do the research which led to the *Praecepta*—and when he left suddenly the Count was quite upset, though I reckon he had other things on his mind, such as the disappearance of the family collection of Barnasite icons.

Creating a character matters; you need to know your characters inside and out, what they ate for breakfast, what they look for when buying perfume for their mistresses, which diseases they had when they were children, all that sort of thing. I'm lucky; as soon as I think someone up, I know him intimately. I don't have to speculate or ask myself, is this or that right for this person. I just know. Which is why I knew the professor would've bought a wool gown as soon as he got off the boat (the Echmen feel the cold so badly in the West) but would insist on keeping his wooden-soled sandals, because no matter how well made, leather soles never feel right and make his back hurt.

"Where the hell," she wanted to know, "are we going to get Echmen sandals from?"

"Attention to detail," I told her.

"Yes, but who's going to notice?"

"Me."

She argued, but only from force of habit. She knew all about attention to detail. Forgers understand these things. They also know that there's some commodities—the passage of time, for example—that can't be had even for ready money, and you need to find acceptable substitutes. So she made me a pair of Echmen sandals. They were perfect. No good, I told her.

"You what?"

"Too new."

To her credit, I didn't need to explain further. Other men might be prepared to go on a long voyage to a strange land in a new pair of sandals, but not the professor. He'd be set in his ways, and experienced enough to know that no man is more wretched than he who finds himself a long way from home in uncomfortable shoes. He'd have worn his favourite pair, properly broken in, so perfectly adjusted to the shape of his foot that he didn't know he was wearing them.

To simulate the effects of three years of daily wear, she gouged out shallow slots in the soles, soaked and dried them to open the grain, then polished them glassy smooth with ten different grades of carpenter's sand, applied on a wooden strickle, followed by buffing soap. She frayed the leather straps with the edge of a razor, just enough to take the square off the edges, and stained them with vinegar to simulate sweat. In fact, it was her idea to roughen the underside of the soles—which don't show and nobody but me would ever have anything to do with—because an Echmen academic would do a lot of walking on pavements, and in the city the doctor came from, the streets are paved with volcanic tufa. If she wasn't scarier than a cave full of tigers, I'd like her a lot. She has a strain of integrity that I can't help but admire.

THE SCAR LEFT by that stupid arrow is one of my very few distinguishing marks, and of course you have to peel my shirt off to see it. Unfortunately it's recorded in vivid detail in the files of criminal investigation agencies right across the world, which is why I keep my shirt on even when it's baking hot. Whereby hangs a tale. There was this man in, I think, Mezentia who was pretending to be me in furtherance of some illegal scheme or other—I assume money was involved, but I don't know the details—and he'd read the files and knew about the scar. There was no real need to worry about it. There was an outside chance he'd have to seduce the wife of the Dean of Humanities, but she wasn't likely to know what was in the police files. Aside from that, no real issue. But this man knew about attention to detail and the vital importance of being in character, so he got an arrow, with a bodkin head like the one I'd been shot with, and fixed it to a door pointing out at right angles, and pulled the door towards himself sharply, impaling himself in the precise spot where I'd been hit. He healed up pretty well to begin with, but then something must've got in the wound, because he went down with gangrene and died.

I suppose it's a bit like religion. Perfect virtue, they tell us, can be achieved only by imitating in every detail the life of the Invincible Sun in His human incarnation; which is why nobody can be perfect, since in order to do that you'd need to be able to die for the sins of the people, be resurrected and ascend bodily to Heaven in splendour. Do not try this, as the saying goes, at home. There's a level of perfection that's unattainable *by*

definition. He can do it, you can't, so don't bother trying. To which I responded at an early stage by saying;
if I can't be perfectly virtuous, I'll always be imperfect,
therefore sinful and wicked, and once I've conceded
that it's all just a matter of degree, which really doesn't
interest me, so why bother at all? My tutors got vexed
at me when I pointed this out to them and told me I
was missing the point. I got the point all right. When
they say, you're missing the point, it means they know
their position is logically untenable. The joker who
pretended to be me did everything right, in terms of
fastidious authenticity, but he died and wasn't able to
resurrect himself. I didn't die. And when I did, I rose
again from the dead. Not that I'm drawing a parallel.
Just something to think about.

I hope you'll understand what I'm getting at when
I tell you that the scar on my chest was, as far as I was
aware, the only clue I'd left open. Everything else that
was possible to cover in advance, we covered. So why
omit the scar? I know it sounds stupid, but when I really
immerse myself in a character I can go in so deep, I need
something—like the golden thread in the Labyrinth
myth—to find my way home with. So long as I had the
scar, I'd know who I really was.

"That's stupid," she told me.

"I know."

"Something like that could get us both hung."

"Yes."

"It's vanity, that's what it is. It's you saying, I'm so
smart, I can leave a bloody great big clue lying about and

still you're too dumb to catch me. It'd be like me signing my work on the back in tiny letters."

But she'd done that, several times, and got away with it. Well, I'd noticed, but nobody else. "I agree," I said. "But I'm superstitious."

"The hell you are."

"It's *like* being superstitious," I said. "And anyway, do you know any way to get rid of a twenty-year-old scar?"

"There isn't one."

THE RECTOR OF the University, no less, introduced me to the Duke and his court at a reception for the Lurian ambassador. The Doctor, he explained, had come to town to examine some ancient and incredibly rare medical treatises in the Palace library. He'd brought with him letters of introduction and accreditation from his own faculty back in Echmen, together with recommendations and testimonials from a dozen world-famous universities, all of which had been duly lodged and declared acceptable by the Abbot and chapter, who'd invited him to lecture to them on Saloninus' theory of the circulation of the blood.

The Duke said he'd heard about that, though he had no idea what it meant. I explained it to him. He was shocked. You mean it goes round and round inside you, he said. Yes, I told him, like irrigation channels or the works of a water-clock. But surely you'd feel something, he said, a sort of throbbing, and a sloshing noise. The human body, I told him, is a remarkable thing. Yes, he said. Quite.

Then I was shoved in front of a few more deadheads, and then the Lurian ambassador, who startled the life out of me by greeting me in practically flawless Echmen, though he did get a couple of the tones wrong. His posting before last, he explained, was as diplomatic attaché to Hocha, on the border between the Sashan and the Echmen, and while he was there he learned the language.

You speak it very well, I told him. He was pleased. Do you really think so, he said.

After that, we got on like a house on fire, and since nobody else in the room could understand a word we were saying, we ended up in a corner of the room, quiet so we could hear ourselves think and handy for the food.

"It must be awkward for you," he said. "I mean, there's hardly anything here you can eat."

I smiled. "Our dietary laws aren't nearly as strict as people think. Besides, even if you're ultra-orthodox, you can eat pretty much anything you like so long as you sanctify it first."

"Excuse me?"

"With *cha* powder," I explained.

"I don't think I ever came across—"

"Ah." Mock furtive. "It's not something we tell foreigners about."

"Oh. So what—?"

"*Cha* powder," I told him, "is the seeds and flowers of a dozen holy herbs, dried and ground and then blessed by the monks of the Crystal Sky monastery, on the slopes of the Holy Mountain. A few specks of *cha* purges all trace of abomination, so you can eat any food that's put in front

43

of you. Provided," I added, "that your motive in doing so is to spare offence to your host, or extreme starvation. Just liking how the stuff tastes won't do, unfortunately."

"That's—ingenious," he said, carefully not grinning.

I shrugged. "As you know," I said, "causing offence to a host or social superior is one of the worst things you can do in our culture. And we found out the hard way, there's few things more likely to upset someone than telling him the delicious food he's prepared for you specially is unclean and an abomination, and just being in the same room with it puts your immortal soul in jeopardy. Also," I added, "our Heavenly Father gave us the Law before we'd made first contact with the Jens Servida."

He nodded gravely. *"Edomi sako."*

"Precisely. But we know that the Heavenly Father is a benevolent god and would never have forbidden us to eat raw fish if He thought that would mean missing out on *edomi sako* marinaded in sweet white wine. So, obviously, there must've been a misunderstanding. Our Father's word is immutable, but the human prophets who recorded it were fallible mortals, after all. And the Jens are such touchy people. They take offence at the slightest little thing."

He was looking over my shoulder. The Duke had a Jens chef working for him, and on a silver platter not six feet from my elbow was a whole *edomi* fish, studded with cloves and so far untouched. The Lurians also have a taboo against raw fish.

"I must confess," the ambassador said, in a slightly husky voice, "in the privacy of my own family circle, I have very occasionally... But at a public function, with people watching—"

From my sleeve I took a little ivory box. She'd made it, because you can't buy really good quality Echmen ivory in the West, and the doctor wasn't the sort of man who'd keep his *cha* powder in any old rubbish. A man with few possessions, but those possessions all of the very best. "You put me in a difficult position," I said. "For me to indulge in a delicacy knowing that my host's honoured guest is forbidden to join me would be appallingly bad manners." I twirled the box in my fingers and put it away again.

"That's it, is it? *Cha* powder?"

Portrait of a man to whom an idea has just occurred. "You don't suppose—" I stopped myself. "I'm sorry," I said. "Please ignore me."

It's the colours that make *edomi sako* irresistible; the glistening orange wrapped round the satiny white, and the little yellow and red bits. Personally I can take it or leave it alone, but true connoisseurs of the stuff just can't get enough of it. A fat man, I think he was the Duke's brother-in-law, stopped and hovered round the plate for a moment before helping himself to pigs' knuckles and fermented cabbage. "One of the purposes of my mission to this country is to help foster ecumenical unity and mutual respect and understanding between people of different faiths."

"Is that so?"

"Absolutely. Our Patriarch feels that now is the time for all people of faith to embrace their similarities rather than their differences."

"To reach out, in other words."

"Oh, I think so, don't you?" He watched me take out the box and slide back the lid. "Just a sprinkle on the top?"

"You can barely taste it."

He darted towards the food table like a squirrel chased by a dog and grabbed a plate. I handed him the box. "Is that enough?" he asked.

"Maybe just a trifle more."

The fish looked like it had dandruff. "Not for me," I said, when he waved the platter at me. "Truth is, I love it but it doesn't like me. Too oily. I'd be up half the night."

All the more for me, then, he didn't say. We carried on chatting for a while after that. Apparently, Lurians don't think it's bad manners to talk with your mouth full.

SHE WAS ANGRY with me. I felt hard done by.

"It's not what I told you to do," she said, accurately. "I told you—"

"Same outcome," I argued. "He made an exhibition of himself, throwing up all over the Duke and Duchess, and he's been sent home in disgrace for breaking Lurian dietary law. He's out of your life. No longer a problem."

"I told you to kill him."

"I don't do that."

Not a word about how clever I'd been, dusting the *edomi sako* with a monster emetic rather than poison. The ambassador's violent reaction had been attributed to the raw fish, and the circumstances made it impossible for him to deny that he'd been eating forbidden food, so there was no choice but to send him home. Nobody dead. Nobody under suspicion of murder. And still she was giving me a hard time.

"It was a big risk," she said. "What if he hadn't been a greedy pig with a taste for exotic food?"

"I understood his character."

"You'd never met him."

"No," I told her, "but I'd heard a bit about him. Enough to know that he was the sort of Lurian who likes going abroad because you can do things there which you can't get away with at home. The rest I extrapolated from what I knew. And guess what, I was right. I don't take risks," I added. "I play carefully calculated odds. There's a difference."

She scowled at me. I was in trouble. So what?

"Anyhow," I said, "I've done what you wanted, so that's all right. It's been lovely seeing you again, and now I think I'll be moving on. I rather like the good Doctor and I fancy he might turn out to be lucrative. Don't worry about my share from the scam, whatever it is. You keep it. I have an idea—"

"You're not going anywhere."

That's one of the things about her. You think she's through with you and you're finally free and clear, but there's always one more trivial favour to be done. "Don't be silly," I said. "You wanted me to get rid of the Lurian ambassador—"

"That was just the start," she said. "There's a long way to go yet."

47

I'd tried to meet her halfway. I'd saved her all the hard work and trouble of double-crossing me and ripping me off for my share by telling her I didn't want it. "There's more."

"Ever such a lot more, yes. All we've done so far is groundwork."

I sighed. "Oh come on," I said, "be reasonable. You can see I don't want to do this."

"You don't even know what it is yet."

"It's something with you involved. That's enough."

For that I got the sort of look that dissolves the enamel off your teeth, and which I've gotten used to over the years. "That's not a very nice thing to say. And I need you."

"No you don't."

"Yes I *do*."

There are ways for a woman to say *I need you, yes I do* to a man that'll break your heart or flood it with joy. And there are other ways. Same words, very different effect.

In case you were wondering, no. Strictly professional, throughout an association going back many years. The way it works is, we bump into each other, we collaborate, she lands me in ghastly trouble and makes off with the proceeds of our joint venture. In the past I worked with her solely because I happened to have a price on my head in the various jurisdictions where we happened to be at the time and she didn't, giving her a certain degree of leverage. Latterly she'd made herself desirable to the authorities in almost as many places as I had, so I'd sort of hoped that her hold over me had dissipated, but apparently not.

"What," I asked her, "could you possibly need me for?"

EVERYTHING IS MY fault.

I started off in the theatre to help out some friends of mine. We were all young and stupid, and they'd pooled what was left of their inheritances to take the lease on the Curtain theatre in Choris Anthropou for the summer season. Dabbling in theatrical management when you don't know exactly what you're doing is the quickest way to get rid of money that doesn't involve fire or deep water, but they thought they'd be fine because one of them was drinking pals with one of the actors in the Duke's Company, and this actor swore blind that he could persuade Theudahad to write a brand new comedy for the Curtain. Put like that it wasn't such a stupid idea. Theudahad had three plays running in Choris that season, all to packed houses, and he'd just fallen out with the Duke's men over who paid what for new rush matting for the floor of the pit.

Sadly, it didn't happen that way. One of the three plays the Great Man had on that year was *The Whore's Tragedy*. Enough said. Theudahad was arrested for sedition and blasphemy, and shortly afterwards drew the biggest house in the shortest run of his career when he starred in his own execution. Which left my pals with an expensive theatre, seventeen actors, forty-six backstage operatives and no play.

So I wrote them one. I did it to help them out, as a bit of fun, because I'd always fancied having a go at it, because I've always felt the drama is the most immediate of the literary genres, because one of the young idiots had a mother who had a particularly valuable piece of jewellery hidden in a chamber-pot under her bed (where a thief would never think of looking, her son proudly informed me) and I wanted to be invited to her house, and because I naturally assumed that if the play was a success they would pay me some money. I wanted to call it *The Worms and the Lions*, but one of them thought *Apis and Sophrosyne* was a much better title, and he was quite right.

Ah well. I was talking to a man a year or so back and he told me he was just returned from Chaxaris. There's no reason why you should have heard of the place; it's some way east of the eastern border of the Echmen empire, and only a few diplomats and very enterprising traders have ever made it out so far. But, this man told me, he went for a stroll round the capital city one evening and what did he find but a theatre playing a Chaxar translation of bloody *Apis and Sophrosyne*, and doing pretty good business too. Every day, in some part of the world or other, someone's staging a production of the wretched thing, and I never see a penny. Personally I think it's a typical young man's play, all rhetoric and tricks and gags, precious little depth or insight into character, but what do I know?

I spent money I hadn't got on lawyers to try and gouge something out of my erstwhile friends, who were now rich enough to afford better lawyers than I could. That got me nowhere, and I never did scrounge that dinner invitation I'd been angling for. On the other hand, every manager in Choris wanted me to write a play for him, and I was only too happy to oblige. It wasn't like it was hard work or anything. All I had to do was choose a plot from some masterpiece I admired by somebody dead, beat it a bit out of shape so that the theft wasn't immediately obvious, decide who the characters were going to be, get to know them, and write down what they wanted to say to each other. That's all there is to it. Anybody who tries to tell you that writing plays constitutes work is lying to you. Essentially all you're doing is eavesdropping on your imaginary friends, pausing now and then to refill your inkwell. Until you've written half a dozen, of course, at which point it all goes blue on you terribly quickly, but I'm getting ahead of myself. For a while there, I honestly believed I'd found my place in the world. True, I wasn't making very much money, about the same per month as a middling competent plasterer working on a government project, because the managers got all the rights. That's how it goes when you're starting in the profession, until the day comes when your name carries so much weight that you can turn round and say no, from now on it's a share of the gross, plus the rights revert to me at the end of the run. I was just approaching that point when one of my other sidelines suddenly went sideways and I found myself leaving Choris in something of a hurry, on a dung cart, cunningly disguised as part of the dung.

You'd have thought that was the end of my dramatic career, but you know what they say, you can't keep a good man down. Within five years my plays were everywhere, filling theatres in places I daren't set foot, making fortunes for people I'd never met, and a particularly daring and imaginative syndicate of managers from Lonazep City tracked me down—I was living in a semi-derelict croft on the north coast of Aelia, dining on hazelnut stew and crab-apples and putting the finishing touches to *Human, All Too Human*—and suggested that I might care to write them something. There wouldn't be an awful lot of money, they explained, because of all the risks and difficulties; me being a wanted man in practically all the kingdoms of the earth might disincline people to see my plays, and then there were all the associated problems of laundering the money so it could be paid to a convicted criminal in a faraway jurisdiction, stuff like that. They mentioned a figure. It was a week's rent in Lonazep, but in north Aelia, if ever I wanted change they'd have to take on extra staff at the mint. So I wrote them *Evil for Evil*, and *Florian IV parts 1 and 2*, and the rest of the histories, and most of what you would know as the City comedies. They called at intervals to collect the manuscripts, and I asked them how the plays were doing and they shrugged and said business was steady, nothing spectacular, you understand, but building slowly. Any chance, I said tactfully, of a bit more money? And they pulled sad faces and didn't reply, so I didn't push it. Eventually a bounty-hunter got the idea of trailing them, leading to a hectic couple of hours for me, followed by a long sea-voyage and three months in a condemned cell in Paraprosdocia, from which I escaped, I kid you not, thanks to a timely earthquake. But that was the end of what scholars call my Aelian period. I wound up in one of the provincial capitals of the Sashan Empire, where theatre is forbidden by law, and decided to explore other avenues.

The Lonazep syndicate, for what it's worth, decided to invest their profits in real estate and built a chain of cities from Chaon in the north right down to the Blemmyan border. You can if you wish reflect on how their dishonesty did them no good in the long run; after a while their oppressed tenants rose up, lynched them and stuck their heads on pikes, and that's how the Caelian Republic was born, so if you're a Caelian you've got me to thank, in a way. For my part, I never got any of the money but my head's on my shoulders, not a pike. I've done a shedload of stupid things in my time, but I've never gone into theatrical management. Too risky.

"I NEED YOU," she told me, "to write a play."

I closed my eyes. Somewhere, in the streets below our balcony, a flower-seller was yelling about fresh violets. "Oh come on," I said.

It turned out that she'd been at the auction where they sold the manuscript of *Philemon and Baucis* for nearly a million. It had given her ideas.

As a trial run, she sold a simple love sonnet. I was rather touched to find she'd kept it until she explained that she'd used it as a bookmark and forgotten it was there until it suddenly fell out at her. I took it as an omen, she told me, having it turn up like that out of the blue. She put it in an auction in Choris and it made fifty thousand; a nice little score (in her exalted terms), just about right for financing the really big score which had suddenly and unexpectedly manifested itself in her mind like the Transfiguration.

If someone was prepared to pay half a million for *Philemon*, she argued to herself, what wouldn't they pay for a brand new, hitherto undiscovered masterpiece? Especially since the man himself was dead, and so everyone had more or less resigned themselves to there not being any more plays, ever again. Think about it, she urged me. We get two million, at the very least, for the manuscript. On top of that, we reserve fifty per cent of the performing rights for the play itself. It really is the big score, she told me, with what might just possibly have been genuine tears in her eyes; the ultimate, the *ne plus ultra*, the last, best hope for a better tomorrow. And all you have to do—

I held up a hand. "It's a nice idea," I said. "Just one thing. Where do you come into this?"

She looked at me as though I'd just stabbed her. "You what?"

"It's a great idea," I said. "I write a play, in my own handwriting, and I put it up for auction. What do I need you for?"

She breathed out slowly through her nose. "You clown," she explained.

BEING SALONINUS. WHAT about it?

I have never deliberately been Saloninus. It's something that comes naturally to me, I suppose, something

I can't help doing, so that in that sense I can reasonably claim not to be responsible for my actions. I don't get up in the mornings and ask myself, what would Saloninus do next? Which in a way is odd. If it was one of my made-up characters, Philemon or Ardester or that idiotic excuse for a human being Florian IV, I'd have no problem. I ask myself that question, what would Philemon or Florian do next, every time I pick up my pen, and the answer always just comes, like the flowers in spring.

But what would Saloninus do next? You're asking the wrong man. In a way it's like archery. Not something I've ever been much good at, but I've known a few of the really top shots over the years and they've never managed to teach me a damn thing, because when you ask them, how do you do that, they don't know. I just look at the target, they say, really *look* at it, and let go of the string.

In my case, of course, most of the time the string is more or less snatched out of my hand. Someone recognises me, something goes wrong, something is found at the scene that implicates me, and all the ice palaces I've so carefully built up around me shatter and melt, and I'm off on my travels again. I sometimes wonder what would have become of me if only I'd taken to art and science and music and literature before I'd taken to crime. But it didn't happen that way, and I have a nasty feeling that it never could have. If I'd stayed peacefully at home and been very, very good, I suspect the slender golden arrows of inspiration would never have come slanting down out of the sky and hit me. Being Saloninus, this far at least, has been thirty per cent pure gold and seventy per cent mixed shit, but it seems almost inevitable that the shit had to come first before the gold could begin to crystallise. I speak, mark you, as a leading alchemist.

So; being Saloninus, as far as I'm concerned, is about reacting desperately to desperate situations. I have this theory about, among other things, coal. I believe that what we call coal is in fact the decomposed compost formed by billions and billions of leaves, which fell long ago from forests long since cleared away; coal is just leaf-mould, compressed over inconceivably long periods of time by the weight of the layers of its own self above it, until it's compacted and squashed almost as hard as stone, made brittle, dry and extremely combustible. There's also evidence to suggest, though I won't bore you with the details, that if you compress the compressed coal long enough and hard enough, that's what makes diamonds. It's just a theory, and I don't suppose you're all that interested. I only mention it because, if it's true, it's a good way to describe the process of being Saloninus. A lot of stuff falls on me from a great height, until the sheer weight of fallen stuff concentrates me very hard indeed, and one of the by-products is flawless gems of great value.

"OF COURSE YOU need me," she told me. "It just won't work otherwise."

It's all a matter, she explained as to an imbecile, of authenticity. You're dead, she pointed out. A freshly-written manuscript, with the ink barely dry, would naturally be taken as a forgery, a blatant attempt to cash in on the latest collecting craze—

"But it'd be genuine," I said.

"Being genuine doesn't matter," she said patiently. "You can be as genuine as a new-laid egg and people will just laugh at you. You've got to *look* genuine."

"Ah."

"That's different. That takes a lot of work."

She knows what she's talking about, trust me. So I paid attention.

In order to *look* genuine, she said, a thing's got to be just right. It's got to be written on the right paper in the right ink, with the right amount of fraying and discoloration, with the right number of spelling mistakes, crossings out, illegible words, whatever. It's got to be—well, *right*. And right, in this context, means it's got to be what people expect it to be.

"But I've only been dead, what, nine months. So it doesn't have to be very old—"

She shook her head, and I realised I was being stupid. "It's got to look like the other manuscripts," she said, "the ones that are proved to be genuine, because their provenances are above suspicion. Otherwise the buyers won't want to take the risk."

"But surely," I said, "the actual play. The words themselves."

Uh-huh. "You don't understand," she said. "The thing of it is, Saloninus is a genius, everybody knows that, but nobody really knows why. Or how, rather. Nobody knows how he does it, or else they'd all be doing it themselves. But about a million people have tried to write like him—"

"Excuse me, but what's with the third person?"

She scowled at me. "It's easier for me, with you sitting there. A million people have tried to write like him but they can't quite do it. It's that indefinable something."

"My point exactly."

"No, you're being stupid, you don't get it. Nobody else can quite do it, but about a million people can get very close. It's a tiny margin, thin as a razor, but so's the difference between being alive and being dead. And nobody's going to bet two million angels on their ability to assess a tiny margin. They say, this reads like Saloninus, but what if I'm wrong? What if I'm too stupid to tell the difference? So instead they go by the handwriting and the age of the paper and the composition of the ink, and most of all by the provenance. Which," she added with a sunrise grin, "is why you need me."

The penny dropped. I once calculated that a falling object accelerates by a fixed ratio of thirty-two feet per second per second; so, the further it falls, the harder it hits when it lands. This penny must've fallen a very long way.

"Oh," I said.

"Exactly. I sold that silly poem of yours and they bought it because everybody knows we used to be lovers—"

"But we—"

"Everybody knows," she repeated firmly. "The provenance was impeccable. So, if you gave me a poem, why not a play?"

Valid point. You know when you're driving a cart through the long grass and you run into a big stone you never guessed was there. She'd got me.

"The reason we're here," she said, in her dove-like cooing voice, "is because— All right. Guess who bought the *Philemon* manuscript."

"No idea."

"The Duke," she said. "Who also bought your crummy sonnet. He's a collector. He's *the* collector. His idea is to build up a massive collection of all the most important manuscripts ever, so that when he's dead people will call him Sighvat the Learned or Sighvat the Wise instead of that bastard Sighvat. We're here so that I can sell him the play. Which he'll buy from me, because he's already bought one absolutely genuine Saloninus manuscript from me, so he knows it's all right."

I felt like I did the first time I saw the pea emerge from under the wrong shell. "I get you," I said.

"Of course," she went on, "before he actually parts with the money he'll have it gone over by experts. Handwriting experts, manuscript experts, historians, scholars and literary critics, the whole nine yards. So it's got to be perfect."

"Well, it will be, won't it?"

She sighed. "You obviously don't understand the first rule of forgery and faking. For a fake to be accepted as genuine, it's got to be better than the original. Not almost as good, not close enough for country music; better. That's always worked for me."

I lifted my head and looked at her. "Better?"

PERFECTION. THAT OLD thing.

We touched on this earlier. Perfection, so they taught me at the seminary, is an attribute unique to the Divine. Only the Invincible Sun is perfect. Our path to salvation is to imitate the divine, but it's an unattainable ambition, a hiding to nothing. So, you can be like me and refuse to play a game where you're not allowed to win, or you can spend your life trying, because success doesn't matter, trying does.

In my defence I've never tried to write the perfect play, symphony, meditation, homily, equation or treatise. I know I can't do it, because it can't be done. I've come close, but so does the man who jumps off a high tower aiming for the three-foot square well of deep water two hundred feet below him. He misses, by a matter of a few inches, and they scrape what's left of him off the flagstones. A nine is a nine is a nine, and when you need to score ten, it's completely useless. The smaller the margin by which you miss, the worse you feel.

I don't aim at the ten. I don't aim at all. I just close my eyes and relax my fingers. And, by and large, I haven't done so terribly badly. With my eyes shut, I outscore everyone else. Comparative merit, as opposed to absolute, is good enough for me. The problem arises when you ask me to compete against myself.

I'd far rather you asked me to create something perfect. At least I'd know what the outcome would be, which would save the anxiety and the stress, and there's always

a chance of getting on a side-bet that I'd fail. But ask me
to outdo myself—see above, under archery. In order to
do that, I'd need to know how I do this stuff in the first
place; what that tiny margin between me and everyone
else actually is. Know your enemy; it's the golden rule
of competition. But the one competitor you can't watch
like a hawk is yourself. I can tell you in exquisite detail
how Theudahad and Simmacho and Notker and Ellaeus
wrote plays, their various tricks and devices, the second-
act reveal, Simmacho's jar on the mantelpiece, the double
peripateia, the third-act syncopated false ending. Ask me
about me; not a clue. I just sit there gnawing the end of
my pen and let the characters do the work.

"This is tripe," she told me.

"I know," I said.

She was getting impatient. She was just back from
a morning hanging round at the Duke's court, where it
was getting harder each day to fend off the Duke's fran-
tic enquiries about the genuine Saloninus manuscript she
claimed to have. "If it goes on much longer, he'll send
someone to burgle the house," she said.

"Tell him it's in a safe place."

"He knows that's not true. He owns all the safe places,
banks, temples, abbey treasuries, he knows it's not in any
of them. It's getting embarrassing. He's not the sharpest
knife in the drawer, but sooner or later he's going to start
suspecting something."

I sighed. The play wasn't going well. I was trying too hard, and I kept getting in the way. There was only one thing I could do, so I did it. I got up, crossed to the fire and shoved my manuscript in among the glowing embers.

"Well, that was melodramatic," she said, as the paper blossomed into flame. "Now what?"

"Now I start again," I said. "New plot, new characters, everything."

"Fine."

I sat down and let my head sink into my hands. "As it happens," I said, "I do have another idea at the back of my mind."

She poured herself a large drink. "Go on."

"There's this prince," I said. "He's lounging about feeling vaguely discontented when suddenly his father's ghost pops up. I was murdered, the ghost said, by my brother; you know, the one who subsequently married your mother and siezed the throne. Avenge me."

I looked at her. "And?" she said.

"The prince avenges him."

"And?"

"That's it."

She put down her drink. "That's it?"

"Yes."

"All right, what about the sub-plot?"

"There isn't one."

"Love interest?"

"No."

"Oh come *on*," she said. "You've got to have a love interest. And a feisty, kick-ass heroine. It's the law."

"No," I said. "There's a girl, but he's not in love with her."

"For crying out loud. So what happens?"

"He sees the ghost. After a while, he kills his uncle. Curtain."

"That's it?"

"There's a certain amount of internal debate about morality and the nature of human existence."

She curled her lip. "Padding."

"You say that like it's a bad thing. It's the stuffing people like, not the chicken."

"Padding," she repeated grimly. "No, what you've got there is Act One, Scene One and Act Five, Scene Six. Now go away and figure out the rest of it."

She was beginning to annoy me. "Who's writing the bloody thing, you or me?"

"You know your trouble? You haven't got a clue. You're not just clueless, you're a bottomless pit down which clues fall and are utterly lost for ever. You can't write that. It's garbage."

IT'S A PROBLEM I have. I tease people.

The problem isn't so much the teasing as the corners I back myself into as a result. Having pitched her the outline of what would obviously turn out to be the worst, most boring play in the history of the drama, I was now committed to writing it, or else face her wrath for wasting precious time by burning two-thirds of a play that could've been fixed with rewrites and judicious cutting. The burning, of course, wasn't the tease. I had to do that, or else I'd have carried on tinkering with the stupid thing when it was obviously dead.

But I've found, on the rare occasions when I'm having difficulties with something, that it often helps to make it harder still. It concentrates the mind, piles on the dead leaves and narrows the focus. Having created for myself the once and future piece of shit, I now began to see its possibilities.

At the very least, I had a character I could listen to. When he first comes on, he's feeling rather like I was feeling at that moment; depressed, miserable, resentful, angry. Then enter the ghost, who immediately multiplies his troubles by a thousand. I paused and listened, and my prince started talking to me.

I listened. I may have chewed the end of my pen a bit. And then it was finished.

As soon as my work ended, hers began. There was nothing I could do to help except keep out of her way, so I sat in a chair and watched. There's something about watching a true master at work that really gets me, especially when I'm not seeing it in a mirror.

We'd figured out that I must have written the play about twelve years earlier, about the same time as the sonnet. In which case, I'd written it in Ap'Escatoy, when I was living in a room over a stable on North Street. Important; because the kind of paper they use in Ap'Escatoy is made from reed pulp, not boiled-rag mush. It's a different colour, the fibres are coarser, and ink doesn't soak into it in the same way. If we used rag paper it wouldn't be absolutely fatal, since it was conceivably possible that I'd written the play on imported paper, maybe a supply I'd brought with me, but it was just the sort of thing that raises an expert's hackles, and once he thinks there's something funny going on, he's apt to pay closer attention.

But it was no big deal. There's only one kind of reed that's suitable for making paper, but fortuitously it was the kind that grows wild along the banks of the river. The actual manufacture makes your arms ache like death but it's scarcely catapult science. Drying the paper once we'd made it was a bit more problematic, since the sun is so much hotter down south; it gives the finished product a crisper feel, and it's shinier. We fixed that by warming it very carefully over a whale-oil stove and burnishing it with a polished steel rod.

Next came the actual writing out—

"What the hell do you think you're doing?" she said.

"Copying—"

"Give me that." She snatched the pen out of my hand. "And get out of my chair. No, don't stand there, you're in my light."

We couldn't use my handwriting. It's always been poor verging on catastrophic, though I'm used to that, but I hadn't realised it had changed over the last twelve years, not till she told me to write something, and then showed me an old letter (the one enclosing the sonnet). I saw what she meant. It was only a slight difference—a bit more rounded, a bit more slipshod—but if you knew what you were looking for, you could see it. And there was no way I'd be able to imitate it. She was going to have to do that. Just as well she's the greatest living expert.

"And I'll do it much faster than you could," she told me, as her hand scuttled sideways across the page like the world's daintiest crab. "That's the trick, go fast. It's when you stop to think that it goes blue on you."

I sat and watched her for a long time. Then she called me over. "I need you to sweat," she said.

"Excuse me?"

"You sweat when you write. Buckets. Didn't you know that?"

No, but I didn't say anything. "So what?"

"I need a couple of drops on this page. And I don't sweat."

Now that I could attest to. "Can't you—?"

"No. You need the real thing. Salt solution ages differently, it's the wrong colour."

So I had to go outside, in the freezing cold, and run round and round the block. "Is that the best you can do?"

"On demand? Yes." I captured a little sweat off my forehead on the tip of my fingernail and trickled it onto the page where she showed me. "That's not quite right," she said. "That's a dribble, not a drop. A drop's round, and that's more pear-shaped. Still, it's done now."

It was strange to see my words being written out in my handwriting by someone else. It would probably have been slightly easier if it had been a stranger rather than someone I knew so well. I offered to dictate to her so she wouldn't have to keep looking from one page to another, but she said no, that would actually make it harder and slow things up. I wasn't sure I liked that. It would have been nice to have played some part in the process. As it was, it felt like I was watching my identical twin brother screwing my wife.

THE THIRD, NO, sorry, the fourth time we worked together, we did what lovers do, up to a point. Between us we created a new life.

The impetus or motivation was a strip of second-rate pasture on the south-facing slopes of the Blackmoor hills, about fifteen miles west of Bine Sauton. When I went to look at it, there was nothing there except a vast, billowing tangle of briars, so tall they choked the few maiden birches and withies; but the underlying soil was sandy loam, and you only get thick briars on good, fertile ground. My guess was that it had once been a vineyard, that if it hadn't it should have been, and that if you found the right buyer, it was worth a great deal of money.

And nobody owned it. I went round asking the locals, and they all shrugged and said, nobody. The district had once been government land, parcelled out to military veterans as their pension, but this particular bit I had my eye on wasn't shown on the government distribution plan in the archive at Bine; nor did it show up on any of the tithe maps at the manor court at Cophis, where the local big house used to be, before it burned down. It quite genuinely didn't belong to anyone.

This sort of thing does happen, very occasionally. Government land gets that way when an estate gets confiscated, for treason or some other major felony; and where you have government action you get government clerks, and for some reason the government doesn't invariably hire the brightest and the best. Mistakes happen, bits get left off, red lines get drawn on plans with a thick brush (and the width of a brush-stroke, to scale, can be as much as a quarter of an acre). My vineyard was probably someone's momentary lapse of attention. It didn't belong to anybody, and Nature abhors a vacuum.

Since I really didn't want to spend the next ten years digging up bramble roots, I decided to sell it. In order to do that, however, I needed to be able to prove legal title. That meant documents. Documents meant a forger. And only the very best would do for the young, stupid Saloninus.

Ownership implies an owner. Abandoned property implies an absentee owner. We conceived and gave birth to one, and then we killed him. Because she insists on doing everything properly, we started with a birth certificate. We decided that our owner had been born in the Sashan empire (because their documents of record are baked clay tablets rather than bits of paper, and baked clay is the easiest written medium to forge, bar none), which meant he had to be the son of a diplomat, posted abroad at the time of his son's birth. In which case, the grant of government land would have been part of his father's retirement gratuity; so after she'd finished the Treasury conveyance, she forged the old man's will, plus an assent to transfer the land from his executors to his son. After that, she did a lovely job of the owner's own death certificate and will, leaving everything to his beloved niece. I wanted it to be to his beloved niece and nephew, but she pointed out that I was a felon, convicted in absentia, and anything left to me in a will would automatically forfeit back to the Treasury. I hate it when she's right.

We sold the land without any trouble at all, and celebrated our triumph with a bottle of vintage Sauton claret. I woke up three days later with a murderous headache; she, of course, was long gone and so was the money. How she got the knockout drops into the sealed bottle without piercing the pitch I really don't know. I've asked her many times, but she just smiles.

The point being; if you go to Bine and consult the records, you'll find irrefutable evidence of the life and death of one Medeis Oudemia, Vesani citizen, born AUC 1018, died AUC 1061. He's a historical fact, with far more documentation to corroborate his existence than, say, Three-Fingers Speusippa or Volusian the Great. She and I created him, sure, but so what? Your mother and father created you. Not only did he have a verifiable existence, he also lived his life with a definite sense of purpose, which is more than I can say for myself, and even after his death he went on helping people. In my darker moods I like to think of him, contentedly pruning his vines in the cool of the evening, watching the sun go down on another useful and productive day.

Since then, with Oudemia very much in mind, I've tried to reconceive myself, loads of times. Scripture says that the only way to escape death is to be reborn, and I can see the sense in that; it's also a good way of avoiding jail time and substantial accumulated debt. It's never worked, though, and I think I know why. The old saying goes, you can't take it with you. I've come to the conclusion that that's right. And where I screw it all up is trying to take myself with me when I go.

FINISHED, THE MANUSCRIPT looked scruffy; a pile of dog-eared, mildewed paper. The damp had got into it so the pages were slightly crinkled, meaning that when it was stacked up it didn't sit true and square. It was tied up with a bit of green ribbon, faded on one side where it had been exposed to the sunlight. It was the sort of thing you'd put out for the rag-and-bone man, or use to light the fire if you were thriftily inclined. It was her master-piece, the best thing of its kind ever created, worthy to be displayed in the company of Prasithon's *Sun Ascendant* or the colossal bronze horse of Prosper of Schanz.

The words weren't all that bad, either. I wasn't entirely sure about some of it. I hadn't been in the sunni-est of moods, and there were places where I'd let myself go rather, mostly in soliloquy form. I've had a lot of stick about my soliloquies over the years; self-indulgent, break-ing dramatic illusion, slows down the action, doesn't advance the plot. Maybe the criticism's valid, I really don't know. Apart from that, though, I was broadly satis-fied with the thing, and I reckoned I'd made my point.

I'd taken a lousy plot with no dramatic potential and made a drama out of it. That, I felt sure, was exactly the sort of thing Saloninus would've taken great pleasure in doing twelve years ago, when he was experimenting with form versus substance and taking delight in doing things he knew would annoy his more sententious critics.

"We've got a product," I said.

"Don't poke at it," she said. "I've arranged it just right. It looks—"

"Real?"

She wrinkled her nose. "You don't want it looking too real," she said. "Too real is usually fake. What you actually want is nondescript."

The nondescript manuscript. Quite. But I could see what she meant. In context, what we wanted was something that had been mouldering in a windowsill for twelve years, forgotten about and uncared for, a piece of junk. That was what she'd so exactly captured. Only a genius could do that.

I couldn't resist asking. "What did you think of it, by the way?"

"Think of what?"

"The play."

"Oh, that." She pulled a little face. "It's a bit long, and the second act drags, and I don't like *him* at all. And the women weren't convincing. To be honest, you've never been much good at female characters."

"Apart from that?"

"The comic gravedigger was a mistake. And I didn't like the ending much."

71

"Apart from that."

"I liked your early stuff better."

You can see how I nearly fell in love with her once.

WE FOUND THE perfect bag in the flea market. It was linen, sort of a sandy colour, with brown stains, dust and fluff trapped in the inside seams and the buckle missing. She put the manuscript in the bag and set off for the Palace.

Now lettest thou thy servant depart in peace. She had no further use for me, and I've found that if I stay in her company for an extended period of time, bad things tend to happen. My instincts told me to slip away quietly, without leaving a note. She'd left twenty-three angels lying around in a locked drawer where anybody could find them. You can go a long way on twenty-three angels.

On the other hand; the big score. If it worked, two *million* angels. There's no generally established exchange rate, but I've always worked on the principle that a million angels constitutes a flight—two million, one each—flights, to paraphrase slightly what I'd just written, of chunky round golden angels sing thee to thy rest, which in my case was long, long overdue. The big score. That much money, even she couldn't be greedy enough to want it all for herself. Not to mention the income from the rights, which on the least optimistic reckoning was likely to be a sum not much smaller than the annual tax revenue of Coele Moesia. It suddenly struck me that if only I hung around a little longer and held my nerve, there was a chance that for the first time in a long and interesting life, I'd actually get paid proper money for something I'd written.

There's a lot to be said for being sensible and one of these days I owe it to myself to give it a go. But (I said to myself; that soliloquy habit again; no good ever came of it) what did I have to lose by hanging around just a little longer? After all, apart from ripping me off (which I was already resigned to, or I wouldn't be contemplating fading away before the money had even been paid over) what else could she do to me? Amend that; what else would she be motivated to do to me, now that I was of no further use to her. It takes positive action to hurt someone, and she'd always been a great one for economy of effort. And in the other pan of the scale was the slight but tantalising chance that this time she wouldn't screw me to the wall and all my troubles would shortly be over.

Give me the choice between doing the right thing and doing the interesting thing, and I'll do the wrong thing every time.

SHE CAME BACK looking stunned. I assumed she'd been mugged, only I couldn't see any blood. How did it go, I asked her.

"He wants it," she said.

"How much?"

"Two and a half million."

There was a long, rather sombre silence. Both of us were thinking the same thing. "Did he haggle much?"

She shook her head. "Two and a half million, I told him. Deal, he said. Then we shook hands."

What we were both thinking was; he would probably have given three. It was one of those thoughts best not put into words.

"Subject to verification, of course," she added, giving herself a little shake, like a wet dog. "I left the manuscript with him. He wrote me out a receipt."

We looked at each other. If anything happened to the manuscript while it was in his custody—fire, theft, mice—he'd be honour-bound to pay us two and a half million angels. And say what you like about him (but not when his spies are listening), he's a man of his word.

"It's the sensible thing to do," I said.

"I know."

"Where do you think he's put it?"

"In the Old Library," she said without hesitation. "He told me so himself. It'll be safe there, he said, and it'll be nice and handy for the scholars I've got coming down from the University. They'll be able to check up references and things without having to traipse across the quadrangle."

The Old Library was, as its name hints, old. Timber-framed. Standing on its own in the middle of the South Quadrangle. A bucket of pitch negligently spilt against a wall; a stray spark from a gardener's negligently tended bonfire.

"Only, why bother?" she said, with a sort of brittle casualness in her voice. "It's perfect. His scholars will pass it with flying colours. Why run all the risk of committing

74

half a dozen felonies when all we've got to do is sit tight and wait for them to bring us the money?"

There are some questions that are never intended to be answered. As for the risk, it was pretty negligible. For someone else, maybe. For me—us—a walk in the park. The blind spot on the east wall was there staring you in the face as you crossed the New Bridge into Parktown. A short dash across the grass, one minute to slop round with the pitch, you'd be back over the wall and safe at your usual table in the *Penitence & Grace* before the glow of the fire was even visible. And the Duke's advisers have been nagging him to replace that semi-derelict fire-trap with a purpose-built home for his valuable books for ages, only he doesn't want to spend the money. Everybody would be far too busy smirking and not saying I-told-you-so to suspect foul play.

But; her masterpiece. Destined to be admired and savagely envied by every guest the Duke ever showed round his collection. Destined to be treasured for ever.

There's a fortune to be made insuring the lives of one's children for substantial sums of money and then murdering them. It's money for old rope and practically risk-free, if you take a few minimal precautions. Even so, it doesn't happen very often, and you can understand why. We looked at each other again. Our baby, we didn't need to say.

"Quite," I said. "Why bother?"

(WHICH WAS STRANGE, because I never feel that way about the stuff I do. Well, maybe some of it, very occasionally. But that's rare. Science I do for money. The same goes for music and plays. There's never been any other reason, as far as I'm concerned. Once the money's in my hand (or not in my hand, as is so often the case) that's it, I'm through with it, all passion spent. Once some eager clown came bounding up to me with a whole load of questions about Cerulion's motivation in Act 3 of *King Axio*. I stared at him, trying to remember which king Axio was, and who in God's name was Cerulion? Simple fact is, I only ever read my stuff once, when I'm writing out the fair copy, and that's it. Can you remember the minutiae of a play you read once, twenty years ago? And I never get to see my plays on the stage, because invariably I'm sitting in a draughty room on the other side of town, frantically writing the next one. Or, when they're revived, I can't afford to buy a ticket.

So I could only guess that the new play mattered to me because she and I had created it together. Not that she'd had anything to do with the words or the order they came in; but at least she'd been there, taking an interest, noticing, asking me what the hell was taking so long. I'm not used to that.)

THERE WAS NOTHING more we could do until the Duke's scholars had looked over the manuscript. We didn't have long to wait.

Over the years—you know how a dog starts barking some time before you hear the footsteps in the street or the knock at the door? I'm like that. Don't ask me how I know, I just do. I wake up in a cold sweat, in pitch darkness and dead silence, I roll out of bed, not bothering with shoes, I grab the bag packed with the absolute essentials, which is always ready and handy so I can find it in the dark without thinking, and I sprint for the escape route, which I'd planned the first time I set foot in the place. A couple of minutes later, when I'm outside and crouching in a shady doorway, the watch or the City guard or the Palace guard come bustling down the street. They pause for a moment to give two or three of their number time to go round and cover the back and sides of the house; then they kick the door in. Once they're all safely inside, I quietly withdraw; walk, don't run, and it always helps if you have at least some idea of where you're headed next. This gift of mine, this sixth sense or whatever, has saved my skin more times than I care to think about, and I've come to rely on it to the point of dangerous complacency.

So imagine my distress when I was jerked out of sleep by someone yelling, *City prefect, open up,* followed by the inimitable sound of splintering wood. I'm not the sort of man who panics, as a rule, but that's because I anticipate, so misfortune rarely catches me unprepared. When it does, I go to pieces, like a covey of partridges all getting up at once.

I slept on the ground floor, under the table she used for work. She slept upstairs, in the bedroom. I knew my escape route wasn't going to be any use to me as soon as I heard the back door yielding to someone's boot. No windows on the ground floor. By the time I'd found my feet, there were steelnecks in the room, waving a lantern around. They saw me. God help me, I froze. I had a nice walnut-sized knob of *gella tonans* in my running-away bag; throw it against a wall and you get a bang, a thick cloud of smoke and a hole big enough to climb through, while the steelnecks are still wondering what hit them. But my bag was on the chair, and there were two guardsmen between it and me. There was nothing I could do. I did it.

"Where is she?" snapped the chief steelneck.

I was debating with myself whether there was any point pretending I didn't know when the lantern lit up the staircase, answering the sergeant's question. Three of them thundered up the stairs. I heard voices, but I couldn't make out the words. Then she came down the stairs, wrapped in a blanket, followed by the guards. She was saying the usual—this is an outrage, the Duke is a personal friend of mine, I'll have your badge for this. The guards were doing the usual, not listening. They formed up round her in the usual formation, marched out through what was left of the doorway and vanished into the darkness. Leaving me behind.

I waited till I couldn't hear footsteps, then five seconds more; then I grabbed my bag and shot out of the back door like a rabbit with a ferret up its tail. Nobody out there. Far away two dogs were barking at each other. It was one of those nights when the moonlight is bright enough to see by even though the sky's overcast—personally I think it's something to do with the light refracting through mist of a certain density, but what the hell—and I had the narrow, high-walled alley entirely to myself. I had no plan of action. Nobody seemed to want me or care about me. I stood there like an idiot until I began to feel the cold, then I went back inside the house and lit a lamp.

I looked at the doors, front and back, but they were both equally beyond repair; the landlord's problem, not mine. I got the charcoal stove going and scrambled a couple of eggs, not that I was hungry but it was something to do. All my instincts were yelling at me to run away, but the idiot who does all the soliloquies kept saying; run away from what? They didn't want you. They had no idea who you are. They think you're dead. Eat your eggs before they go cold.

What was I? Upset? Disappointed? Offended? Nearly the whole of my adult life there have been people only too willing to pay large sums of money for me; for the creations of my brain and hands, for my presence in a locked room, eight feet by six. Actually, no, I wasn't. I was just confused, a rarity for me. Generally speaking, no matter how bad things get, I have some idea of what's going on. At the very least, I know where I need to be, even if it's highly unlikely that I'll get there any time soon. I felt left out, if that makes any sense. I wasn't sure I liked it. It made me feel ordinary.

Cooking isn't one of my talents. The eggs were horrible, like eating that mushy fungus that grows out of rotten trees. I sat down on the chair and waited to see what came next, like a member of the audience.

SOME TIME LATER, enter her; in a man's coat two sizes too big for her, bags under her eyes, no makeup, white as a sheet and furiously angry. There was no door to slam, a deficiency which clearly annoyed her. She looked at me. "You idiot," she said.

I may have dozed off. I looked up and stared at her. "They let you go," I said.

"You clown. How could you be so stupid?"

"Have you had breakfast?" I asked her.

She sat on the chair. I perched on the edge of the table. She burst into tears.

"What happened?" I asked.

"He doesn't want to buy it," she said.

It wasn't the reply I'd been expecting. "Are we in trouble?" I said.

"He isn't going to press charges, because the attorney-general doesn't think there's enough evidence to secure a conviction, but he has serious doubts about my honesty and he'd be obliged if I left the Duchy as quickly as conveniently possible."

At which point I noticed the linen bag, the one we'd bought in the flea market, slung around her neck. She still had the manuscript.

"So we can go," I said.

"What?"

"We're free to leave."

"What? Oh, yes. All that work for *nothing*. And it's all your fault."

Maybe she hasn't spent as much time with steelnecks as I have, I don't know. To me, she sounded a bit like someone who's fallen off a cliff onto a cartful of soft hay, and is yelling at the carter for not taking out a dried thistle. "What happened?" I asked her.

SHE TOLD ME, at length, in detail.

The Duke's experts examined the manuscript. They carefully shredded a tiny sample of the paper, and sure enough, it was reeds, not rags. They tested the ink, which was the basic oak-gall-and-soot mix in which nearly all Saloninus' known manuscripts were written, mixed in the proportions he invariably used. The handwriting man was prepared to pledge his immortal soul that everything was just how it should be—the looped d's, the slanting dots on the i's which characterise Saloninus' middle years (news to me, but then, I'm not an expert), a faint slope of the lines left to right indicative of haste, which you'd expect from a man writing to meet a deadline. Everything—she looked daggers at me at this point—about the manuscript itself was perfect and above reproach. The problem lay with the content.

("Oh come on," I said. "It's probably the best thing I ever—"

"Shut up.")

The difficulties with the metrical form, said the literary experts, weren't insuperable. True, there were seventeen-point-three per cent more lines with feminine endings in this play than in *No Wit Like A Woman's*, its immediate predecessor, but it could be argued that at this point in my career I was being influenced by Macrobian post-realism, and the subsequent decrease in feminine endings merely reflected a rejection of the neo-Classical. Possibly more disturbing was the decline in the number of enjambements—down nineteen per cent from *No Wit*, anticipating the polished fluency of the mature tragedies—

("That's good, surely."

"Be *quiet*.")

Even that (she went on) could perhaps be accounted for by the subject matter, since Saloninus consistently uses enjambement more in the naturalistic dialogue of the City comedies than in the sublime periods of the tragedies. A similar argument could be advanced to account for the comparative infrequency of such devices as paraprosdocia, chiasmus and aposiopesis—

"What the hell," I had to ask, "is paraprosdocia?"

"Interrupt one more time," she said, "and so help me I'll break your arm. Basically, they said, the style was inconclusive. They reckoned something about it stank, but it could just possibly be explained away. What did it for them was the topical reference."

"What topical reference?"

She quoted;

Approach thou like the rugged Aelian bear,
The armed rhinoceros or the Blemmyan tiger,
Take any shape but that, and my firm nerves
Shall never tremble—

"You halfwit," she added. "What were you thinking of?"

"What bloody topical reference?"

"The Blemmyan tiger, of course, you moron. The first Blemmyan tiger to be exhibited outside of its native country was brought to Choris three years ago and put on public display at the New Palace. Everybody went to see it. For a while you couldn't move for paintings of tigers, statues of tigers, tiger wall-hangings, wine-coolers and samovars in the shape of a crouching tiger—"

"News to me," I said.

"Bullshit."

I shook my head. "Three years ago I was in Permia. Up there, they don't even know where Choris is, let alone the latest fashion craze." I stared at her. "Is that it?"

"Yes."

"They say the play's a fake because of some ludicrous stuff about a tiger?"

"It's an obvious topical reference, according to them."

"Like hell it is," I nearly shouted. "Listen. I nearly made it a wolf, but then I thought, tiger's got that slightly exotic feel about it and the line sounds better with the extra foot. They're *wrong*, dammit."

She gave me a look. "Yes," she said, "but we can hardly tell them so, can we?"

It was enough to reduce a man to tears. "Why the hell," I said, "didn't you pick that up when you were copying it out?"

"I didn't know," she said. "I was in Messagene three years ago. I never heard about any stupid tiger."

There didn't seem to be much else to say.

LATER, I TRIED to make the best of it. We've still got the manuscript, I said. We can put it up for auction, some-where else.

"Idiot," she said. "You don't suppose these collectors don't talk to each other, do you? By now, every manuscript fancier west of the Maugrat knows about the Blemmyan fucking tiger. No, what we've got here is three hundred sheets of the most expensive arsewipe in literary history. Nine months of my life, planning it all, finding you, making the stupid thing. Not to mention being dragged through the streets wrapped in a blanket, thinking I was off to the gallows. This is the last time I let you talk me into—"

I wasn't listening.

Cast your mind back to the dropping penny. Now imagine that the penny is one of those rocks that comes screaming down out of the sky and digs a crater the size of a village.

"It's all right," I told her.

When you hunt the wild boar (so they tell me) and the loathsome thing charges you, your only chance of getting out of it in one piece is to plant your spear firmly on the ground, the butt end anchored by the side of your back foot, and point the sharp end at the boar. In its rage and fury, the stupid creature will rush straight at you, not noticing or ignoring the lethal spike between you and him, and impale himself to the heart before he realises something is wrong. She stopped in mid-charge and looked at me. Something in my tone of voice, presumably.

"You what?"

"It's all right," I said. "I can see a way round this. Maybe not quite so much money, but maybe even more."

She knows me quite well. She doesn't like me much, but she knows me. "Are you serious?"

"It'll take a bit of time," I said, and I paused to grin, because an essential part of the idea had just dropped elegantly into place, like a component in a beautiful and complex mechanism. "But there's no risk, hardly any additional outlay, and—well, it's perfect, that's all. Actually, genuinely perfect."

It's not a word I use lightly, for reasons touched on above. But I choose my words carefully, always have.

"Well?" she said.

"Well," I said, "I think we've established that this play isn't by Saloninus. Agreed?"

"You bet agreed."

"Fine," I said. "In that case, it needs to be by some-body else." I smiled. "Somebody better."

When I was a student at the University, I knew a man whose father was the leading icon-painter in the whole of the Western Empire, and he told me a story. His father had been commissioned to paint a small devotional icon for the Duke of Mancalo. The fee was some ridiculous sum, five figures, but my friend's father was the temperamental sort. The agreed subject was the Ascension, but he simply wasn't in the mood. He wanted to paint the Harrowing of Hell, but nobody was in the market for one of those at that precise moment. Never mind, he went ahead and painted it anyway; and meanwhile the Duke's secretary was practically camping out on his doorstep, respectfully clamouring for his master's wretched Ascension.

My friend's father had almost finished his Harrowing, but not quite, and he had a temper and an unconventional sense of humour. He sent his servant down to the Fish Market, where you can always find half a dozen sad-faced men sitting on the ground behind a blanket, on which are spread out a selection of the cheapest, nastiest mass-produced icons money can buy if it's misguided enough to want to do so. Here's twenty stuivers, he said. Buy the first Ascension you see and bring it back here stat.

His servant was an honest man and gave him the five stuivers change. Then, as instructed, he wrapped the icon up in red silk and took it to the Duke. Next day, the secretary called, bringing with him a draft on the Knights of Equity for the five-figure fee (plus a handsome bonus) and a letter—in the Duke's own handwriting, for crying out loud—thanking him for the painting, which was the most beautiful thing he'd ever seen. The only possible thing he could do, the Duke said, was endow a monastery to house it and preserve it for ever.

My friend's father was a bit shaken by this, and he decided to try an experiment. He took down all his very best and finest icons, the ones he hadn't been able to bear to be parted from no matter what he was offered for them. He wrapped them in a blanket and set out for the

Fish Market. By the time the sun set he'd sold two icons and made twenty-seven stuivers.

My friend's father originally rose to the top of his profession on account of a simple mistake. Having no commissions, he painted a series of the Hours of the Passion, twelve in all. At that time, the ruling fashion decreed that only icons painted by monks could possibly be any good, so he signed them Brother Modestus, which was not, of course, his name. What he didn't know was that the Emperor's youngest nephew had recently retired to a monastery and had taken the name Modestus; furthermore, it was widely known that the young prince had been known to dabble in the fine arts. A high-class society dealer saw the paintings, read the signature, put two and two together, bought the lot and promised to pay silly money for more stuff by the same artist. By the time the dealer realised his mistake, genuine art-lovers had acquired a taste for canvasses by Modestus, and my friend's father never looked back.

I rarely if ever look back, because there's always the danger of tripping over your feet while you're running away.

THERE'S A LOT to be said for libraries. Generally they're quiet and restful. You look up from your seat and you see hundreds and thousands of books, each one of them a walled city inhabited by and guarding the informed, the wise, the sympathetic, the understanding. There are friends in books that I've known all my life, with me wherever I go. Libraries are the granary of the spirit, without which we couldn't survive the siege. Some of the books have my name written on the spine or embossed on the brass tube, and because of that I shall never entirely die. Books make you happy, angry, peaceful, discontented, reassured, justified. A book can make me forget who and what I am, for a little while. A book is somewhere I can go and not have to take myself with me. Books say; come to us, all who labour and are heavy laden, and we will give you rest. Books are the islands in the West where good people go when they die. Books are a world apart, yet firmly here and now, written in the moment but eternal; in the beginning was the word, and ever shall be, world without end. Also, some books are very valuable, and the security arrangements in libraries are often woefully lax.

I tried not to think about that. I was in the Old Library of the Studium for a specific purpose, a job to do, no time to be indulging myself and fooling around. I was taking a risk just being there, given that I was dead and buried. I kept a scarf round my face at all times, which itched like buggery and drew unwelcome attention— why would a member of a veiled Order be so interested in modern secular literature?—and whenever I spoke to a librarian I mumbled and avoided eye contact, fortunately not atypical behaviour among scholars. The hell with it. Thirty years since I was here last, and even I'm not that memorable, I hoped.

I have this theory; not one I've ever written up, let alone published, because it's self-evidently false, but that doesn't stop me believing it. I think there are places that are so right for us, at various times of our lives, that we never leave. A small part of us, in my case probably the good part, stays behind, unchanging, for ever. So strongly do I believe this that I was convinced that when I looked up from my desk, I'd catch sight of the young, not-yet-famous, not-yet-fucked-up Saloninus hauling a book down from the open shelves or yawning his way through Priscillian on Oratory. He wasn't there. I can only assume he had a cold that week, or a really bad hangover.

Libraries set me thinking about who the hell I'm supposed to be. They break up the available light like a prism. Who I was; who I am now; who or what, if anything, I shall be. Who I once was but stopped being, who I still am, regardless. Suppose they spread me out on a table and dissected me—a lot of people have wanted to do this—could they identify the various components? A little pile of organs here containing all the bad stuff, the dishonesty, lies, betrayals, cheating, arrogance, cowardice, running away. Another pile next to it; bits containing the science, the philosophy, the plays, the music. Or would they find that the lies and the theories and the tragedies and the thieving were all part of the same thing, impossible to tease apart or smelt or refine with acids; not a library with sections (ground floor, theft, dishonesty and callous treachery; first floor, scientific method and the triumph of reason; art and literature, the mezzanine and the annexe) but all of them words making up one sentence, and if you took any of them out, the whole would no longer make sense? A book can be many things at the same time; a source of enlightenment, a masterpiece of the leather-tooler's art, a handy way to carry two hundred angels in an inside pocket out through the door and down the street to the nearest receiver of stolen goods. You can read me like a book, can't you?

Above all, a library is a place of work. Not much else you can do there. Food, drink, conversation, fornication and falconry not allowed on the premises. A library is a place for diligent study and earnest endeavour. All work and no play makes you a junior assistant lecturer, with tenure.

And libraries don't change all that much, and what they had thirty years ago they probably still have, unless I've stolen it, though they may have forgotten where it's kept. We haven't got that, said the librarians. Yes you have, I told them, go away and look for it, this time properly. They found it. I smiled. Hello, old friend, I muttered under my breath.

THEN IT WAS her turn.

As well as being the best false calligrapher, paper-and-parchment ager, handwriting mimic and bibliophiliac chemist under the sun, she's no slouch at die cutting and seal engraving. We needed a seal; or rather, we needed the impression of a seal, which made life a bit easier.

Your slapdash, born-to-hang cowboy seal-faker gets an impression of the seal he intends to duplicate, usually affixed to a letter or other document. He rolls up a ball of fine-grained clay, presses it onto the seal, peels it off carefully, so as not to distort it, and bakes it in an oven or simply waits for it to dry in the sun. He now has a passable matrix. Press it onto molten wax or lead and you get something that'll fool ninety-nine out of a hundred clerks, jailers and government officials. Any idiot can do it, and most of the people who do it are idiots.

Or you can do it properly. You get a small piece of suitable material. Sandstone is cheap or free, soapstone is the industry standard; she never works in anything but jade. By skill and eye alone you copy the original, chipping and scraping and scribing with tiny steel implements, except that you don't; you make a concave copy of a convex master, which requires powers of visual imagination way beyond anything I could possibly imagine, let alone aspire to. When you've finished, you hold the thing you've made over a candle-flame until its hollow inside is evenly coated with a thin smear of soot. Then you press it down on top of the seal on your letter or document and take it away again. If the original isn't evenly covered in soot, you know you've gone wrong. Probably you have to throw away what you've just made and start again, from scratch. Even if your fake passes the smoke test, there's a fair chance that it'll simply look wrong—identical but different, no bloody use. I've often thought that anyone capable of making a really convincing fake seal must be a fundamentally evil person, because with those skills you could make an absolute fortune doing legitimate work, in which case you're doing bad things for the love of it, not the money.

She's simply the best there is. She has a hollow glass globe about the size of my head, which she fills with water and puts in front of an oil lamp in front of a diptych mirror; the result is fake sunlight, brighter than the actual sun. Most of her scribers and picks are as thin as hairs—she made them all herself—but hard enough to cut stone and tough enough not to bend when she puts her weight behind them. She's got the best eyesight of any living creature, and a lens, which she made by grinding a slab of glass on a potter's wheel covered in sand set in bitumen until it was exactly the right shape; the hardest three days of her life, she told me. I'm amazed she did it so quickly. According to her, with the lens set up just so, the tip of one of those tiny scribers looks as big as a chicken's claw, and as long as you go nice and slow and steady, there's nothing to it, really.

With hindsight, a blob of clay would have done just as well. The clerk who examined the seal in the secretary's office was an old man who had to press his nose against a letter before he could read it, and besides, who on earth would possibly want to fake the seal of the Dean of the Faculty of Secular Literature at the University of Schanz?

I DIDN'T GO to the auction. I'd have liked to, but I'm dead. So I stayed at home and waited.

The final hammer price was four million, two hundred and sixty thousand angels. Just think about that. Enough money to buy all the wheatfields in the Mesoge, or build five thousand ships, or endow fifty monasteries, or fight a land war in Aelia for a week. Payment was by letter of credit drawn on the Order of the Poor Friars, because there aren't 852,000 gold five-angel coins in existence. The buyer insisted on remaining anonymous, but reliable rumour had it that it was either the Sashan emperor, Luomai Met'Oc or the Mezentine Glassmakers' guild pension fund. Nobody else could possibly have afforded it.

How did I do it? Simple.

Very few of my friends have ever done me any good, but in this case I owe it all to my pal the icon-painter's son. He gave me the idea, in roughly the same way the Invincible Sun gave Man the gift of fire, a glowing ember in a hollow fennel stalk.

The Faculty of Contemporary Letters at the Studium hold an annual seminar, at which papers are presented by or on behalf of the most eminent scholars in the Robur-speaking world. That year, the most exciting and controversial offering was an essay by one Segipert, hitherto unknown but vouched for by the Dean of Faculty at the faraway but prestigious university of Schanz.

The title of the paper was; On The Authorship of The Plays of Saloninus.

Marvellous effort, though I do say so myself. Segipert began by posing the obvious question. Was it really credible that an incorrigible small-time thief and confidence trickster could have written the plays that bear his name, not to mention the philosophical treatises, scientific works and musical compositions? Segipert freely admitted that he wasn't qualified to discuss science, philosophy or music, so he'd concentrated his attention on the plays, a subject he knew something about.

In the first part of the essay, he collated vocabulary and imagery that proved that the author of the plays must have had extensive first-hand knowledge and experience of royal courts, diplomacy and the business of government. Saloninus, he pointed out, had none of these, apart from the circumstances of his disastrous first marriage, which were hardly conducive to absorbing a detailed understanding of such issues.

Next he examined various documents written by what he called the historical Saloninus, the man wanted by the authorities in practically every jurisdiction on Earth. To these he applied various philological and metrical tests, from which he drew the inevitable conclusion that Robur wasn't even the historical Saloninus' first language. When he applied the same tests to the plays, he found that not only was the author a native Robur speaker, he was also from one of the three northern provinces of Meturene—the dialectic and syntactical signatures were unmistakeable. Saloninus, the historical Saloninus, had never been anywhere near northern Meturene in his life, as witness the fact that there were no outstanding warrants for his arrest in that jurisdiction.

There followed a summary of the known facts about the life of the historical Saloninus, with particular emphasis on where he was known to have been at the time the plays were composed. In prison; on a prison galley in the middle of the Aelian Sea; a thousand miles away on the borders of the Echmen empire. Unless he had an identical twin brother or wings like a bird, it was simply impossible for him to have written at least four of the twenty-seven plays attributed to him.

Therefore, Segipert argued, Saloninus did not write the plays. In which case, who did?

I waited. Then I waited a bit more. After that, all I could do was wait.

Four and a quarter million angels. More money than anyone could ever spend, or need, or even want. I could imagine my partner ripping me off if it was just a single lousy million. Suppose you split that fifty-fifty. You might feel that extreme bad luck could intervene and wipe you out of a mere five hundred thousand. You might build a city with it, and then there might be an earthquake, the ground opening and swallowing it up. Stuff happens. You'd want to hang on to the whole million, just in case. But four million; four and a *quarter*. Just the quarter would be a bigger score than anything I'd ever played for in my whole life.

Maybe we should have discussed it before she went to the auction, leaving me behind. I should have said to her, straight out; I know you'll double-cross me, and that's fine. After all, the bare bones of the scam were your idea, you did a lot of the work and I did make one tiny mistake, so it's only fair that you should get, say, sixteen-seventeenths of the take. But would it kill you to

spare me just one lousy seventeenth? It would make me
so happy, and think how virtuous and honest it'd make
you feel.

I waited, but she didn't show. It won't hurt, I told
myself, to wait just a little bit longer. That's one thing
you learn when you're dead. Patience.

THEREFORE, SEGIPERT ARGUED, Saloninus did not write the
plays. In which case, who did?

We have already established, he continued, a number
of facts about the true author. He was born and raised
in northern Meturene, he was a man of good family, he
enjoyed a political or diplomatic career. Already, the
field of potential candidates has shrunk to a mere half
dozen. Five of them we can safely discount, for a variety
of reasons. The sixth—the only possible contender—is
Gilifred, Margrave and hereditary Elector of Stammen.

Consider the facts. Gilifred (nicknamed the
Frogmouth) was born at the castle of the Stammenburg
on the border between the central and eastern provinces
of northern Meturene. He was educated at the university of Felsen—of which more later—and thereafter
embarked on a period of service as the Imperial ambassador to Blemmya. On his return he retired to his extensive
estates, where he lived out the rest of his life. He died—
coincidence?—six months before the historical Saloninus.

It is regrettable, Segipert went on, that the main thing
for which Gilifred is remembered today is his appearance.

K. J. PARKER

The Stammen jaw had been a distinguishing feature of his father's family for seven generations. The Lysacht nose, inherited from his mother, Adiol of Lysacht, was always equally prominent. Together, the effect was unfortunate. Fiercely conscious of his disadvantage, Gilifred was throughout his life a solitary, private man, becoming more reclusive as he grew older and the stigmata of his heritage grew more pronounced. He did his duty to his country and his emperor to the best of his abilities as ambassador, but his extreme self-consciousness made him diffident and somewhat remote; a man unable to express himself by conventional means, cut off from the normal society of his equals, perforce an observer rather than a participant; a prisoner of his own body, with no option but to spend most of his life trapped in his own company. He never married. Birth and breeding urged him to distinguish himself, as his forefathers had so spectacularly done in every field of human endeavour. The same thing, the visible legacy of his ancestry, prevented him from doing so. Inevitably, such a man would have to find an outlet, a way of making his mark on the page of history. The desire for fame and glory would have no appeal to a scion of the legendary house of Stammen. Money could not possibly have interested him. But achievement; he would have felt it as a burning physical need. He must achieve, or die. And, since every other avenue was closed to him, where else could he turn but the arts?

Here, once again, his ancestry and family pride at first seemed to thwart him. An Elector of the Empire, writing plays for the public stage; unthinkable. Very well; if he was to fulfil his destiny, he must do so secretly, under an assumed name. Furthermore, there must be no possibility whatever of his secret being revealed. Let it be known that he was dabbling in such things and all his achievements would instantly turn to shame. A dreadful dilemma for a sensitive, tortured man.

At some point, therefore, he will have remembered a chance encounter from his student days. There is firm documentary proof that, while he was a student at Felsen, the historical Saloninus also resided in the town. They both frequented the same inn; we have a sutler's bill, for fortified wine and herrings, addressed to the young margrave; an injunction taken out by the landlord barring the historical Saloninus from his premises on account of breakages and obnoxious behaviour. The two men, therefore, met. Quite possibly, the older man's outrageous conduct, specious glamour and catchpenny wit impressed itself on the impressionable mind of the shy young nobleman. From these facts it is but a short step to an agreement between them, a deadly secret that both would carry to the grave. Gilifred would write plays; Saloninus would pass them off as his own and see that they were produced.

A plausible hypothesis, but can it be proved? Yes, said Segipert, it could, and beyond all reasonable doubt. By good fortune, a number of works from Gilifred's pen survive, preserved in the family archives, which on his death and the extinction of his direct line passed into the custody of the monks of the Studium. They are slight enough, very limited in scope; letters to his father and a cousin; essays on philosophy, theology and the humanities, written while a student; a slim volume, in blank verse, on hare-coursing. But the most rigorous linguistic, grammatical, metrical and stylistic analysis proves beyond any possibility of a question that the man who wrote them *also wrote the plays.* All the most reliable indicia—use of subordinate clauses, incidence of the double caesura, frequency of *hapax legomena* (here followed thirty-six pages of detailed philological evidence, in paralysing detail)—point to the same conclusion Gilifred of Stammen was the true Saloninus.

We are on firm enough ground when we speculate as to the mechanics of their collaboration. Gilifred sent manuscripts to Saloninus, who copied them out in his own semi-literate handwriting and sold them to theatrical managers. In consequence, Saloninus enjoyed his undeserved moment in the sun, while his noble patron had at least the private satisfaction of knowing that, like his forefathers, he had made no small contribution to the wellbeing of all mankind—

THE FIRST THING they take you to see in Apaogoa City is the statue. I went there about fifteen years ago, just to see it—mostly to see it (at that time there was no extradition treaty between Apagoa and the Empire)—and yes, I was impressed.

The statue is fifty feet tall. A woman stands with her arms by her side, looking down from a mountaintop onto the city below. The locals tell you that they don't know who she is, but she's waiting for the world to end.

Clearly a patient woman, because she was there long before the city, which is relatively recent, though built on ruins built on ruins built on ruins... People have lived there for a very, very long time, but not the same people. When I was there, someone had just dug a well. The story was, the well-sinkers were about a hundred and sixty feet down when they came up against what seemed to be solid rock. It was the flat roof of a building. They broke through and realised that their fragile wicker cage was dangling inside a large chamber. Their lamps flashed off gold and silver, but too far away for them to see. They scrambled back up to the surface, got an armful of better lamps, and went down again. They saw the interior of a vast temple, its walls covered with gilded mosaics, its roof-beams supported by exquisite marble, porphyry and alabaster columns. Above a solid gold altar they saw an icon, ten times life size; a mother and child of such transfixing beauty that none of them were able to eat or sleep for days afterwards. They saw inscriptions on the walls, in some sort of hieroglyphic script, hundreds of thousands of words miraculously preserved for who knew how many centuries, representing who knew what sublime and ineffable truths. They saw chests, coffers, reliquaries, pyxes and caskets of gold, silver and ivory, all intact, their seals unbroken. Even the silk hangings around the altar and the gorgeous cloth-of-gold hassocks were perfectly preserved. It was, they later agreed, like a vision of Paradise, and worth an absolute fortune.

They hauled up their basket to the place where they'd smashed through the roof, carefully replaced the fragments of slab and sealed them with lead. Then they rushed into the city to tell various business associates of theirs what they'd found.

It took them a while to raise the sort of capital and make the sort of deal that was needed to do their discovery justice, so it was several weeks before they were able to return. They broke the seals, removed the pieces of slab, lit their lamps and lowered their basket. They went down about six feet, and hit water. The whole place had flooded.

Learned men from the university eventually came up with an explanation. It was something to do with air pressure, the weight of a hundred and sixty feet worth of stone and rubble, the disturbance caused by breaking the roof, a change in the direction of a subterranean watercourse, a little shifting and settling; at some point since the temple was lost and buried one tiny crack in the temple wall, with all that pressure behind it. All good, valid science, I have no doubt. Anyway, that was that. The short version of the story is that a number of men went to dig a well, and they succeeded. They didn't get to achieve the big score, but then again, nobody ever does.

(THE SCHEME WAS, as I explained to her after the Duke's men had let her go, brilliant, foolproof and simple. If the play wasn't by Saloninus, it had to be by someone else. Someone better. Someone worth even more money.

The problem wasn't with the play, or the manuscript. It was the provenance that was no good. But without a provenance, nobody would give her sixpence for it. So we needed another provenance. She had already committed herself to one version of her dealings with Saloninus, which had been proved to be a lie. So we needed a reason for that lie which would make her a credible witness once again.

Easy as falling off a log.

Bear in mind that I first met her, all those years ago, in the Boar's Head tavern in Schanz, where she was working in the hospitality and entertainment sector. She introduced me to a rich and spectacularly ugly undergraduate who was looking for someone to ghostwrite some things for him—essays, letters home begging for money to pay off his debts, that sort of thing. As it happens, I knew him slightly. Everybody in Meturene (where I was born and grew up; never been back since) knew Pigface by sight, and I'd actually spoken to him, begging him not to send my father to the slate quarries for poaching two rabbits. But I forgave him. I even knocked him up a mock-epic about hunting for some dinner-party entertainment he was organising. He was an idiot but we got on quite well together. He paid my bar bills, and gave her a small gold brooch with a tiny chip of genuine ruby.

All of that is true; but the truth gets lost and buried, and when eventually it's dug up again, sometimes it needs to be cleaned and carefully restored, like a neglected work of art. The bit we restored was the bit where she and Gilifred remained friends throughout his life; she knew his dark secret but wild horses wouldn't have dragged it out of her while he was still alive. So, when desperate poverty forced her to sell her most treasured possession, the play he'd written for her, she kept up the pretence that it was by Saloninus. The mistake she made was trying to give it a fake provenance by linking it to the letter the historical Saloninus had sent her, enclosing a sonnet—by Gilifred, of course, but Saloninus had shamelessly copied it out and passed it off as his own. Quite rightly, her attempt at fraud had been frustrated by the Duke's scholars, though of course they only grazed the surface, so to speak. But when Segipert's paper was published and everybody knew the secret, what possible harm could it do finally to tell the whole, unblemished truth?)

AFTER I'D BEEN waiting for a very long time, some steelnecks came and arrested me, acting on information received from a lady, whose name (quite properly) they declined to reveal. They accused me of being Saloninus. I can't be, I told them, he's dead. Prove you're not him, they said. Prove I am him, I replied. Eventually they let me go. While they were at it, they gave me some very wise, valuable advice. Leave town, they said.

SUICIDE IS GETTING to be a habit with me. Unlike most habits, though, I believe it's good for me. I killed Saloninus' body to escape my enemies. I killed his immortal soul, his deathless name, his glory, to be rid of her. Small price to pay.

We're bilingual in Mesurene, even the country people. And, before my death, I wrote twenty-three plays. Even when I lie, I tell the truth. And when I'm telling the truth, I'm generally lying.

I'm not sure what I'm going to do with the rest of my life, but at least I have an opportunity I haven't enjoyed before. I can, if I so choose, go away and leave myself behind; crucified, dead and buried. And if that's not the big score, I don't know what is.